COLD TOM

a novel by
SALLY PRUE

Scholastic Press ∗ *New York*

LIBRARY OF CONGRESS CATALOGING-IN-PUBLICATION DATA

Prue, Sally. Cold Tom / by Sally Prue. — 1st American ed. p. cm.
Summary: Struggling to find a place for himself, Tom flees the elven parents who hunt to kill him and becomes involved with human "demons" in the nearby city.
[1. Elves — Fiction.   2. Identity — Fiction.]   I. Title.
PZ7.P949349   Cal 2003   [Fic] — dc21   2002075802

ISBN 0-439-48268-2
10 9 8 7 6 5 4 3 2 1   03 04 05 06 07

Printed in the U.S.A.
First American edition, June 2003
The text type was set in 12-pt ACaslon Regular
Book design by Dave Caplan

COLD TOM

1

The Tribe fled. Tom, frantic, heaved himself into the purple branches of a scrubby blackthorn and held himself as still as he could.

There were three of them. Demons. Not especially large, these ones, but heavy, hot, gross — blaring at each other with ugly voices.

Tom did his best to quieten his breath. How had demons got here? He hadn't been asleep, he was sure of it. He should have seen them long ago.

They were heading this way. They made enough noise with their trampling — so why hadn't he heard them before?

They were coming back into sight round a tangle of hawthorn, and now he could smell them, musty and foul, spewing frost-clouds into the air. They kept touching each other, holding each other, casting slave-shadows into each other's minds.

Tom held his breath so he wouldn't be sick.

1

They were going to pass right underneath him. Tom's heart was thudding, loud against his ribs. Demons were half blind and half deaf — but they were very close now. The bare branches of the blackthorn were quivering with the tremors of their footfalls.

One of the demons stretched out a heavy arm. It snatched a branch out of its way, and the whole tree heaved and whipped back and Tom's feet slipped. He fell, grabbed, caught something, and hung.

He'd set the birds squawking — but the demons didn't even turn their heads. They trudged on, half deaf, heedless. By the time Tom had found a foothold again all that was left of them was the ugly blaring of their voices.

Tom drew in a long, slow breath and gave thanks to all the stars.

A ruffle passed over the clearing — not much more than a stirring of the fallen leaves — and the Tribe was there again before him. There were a dozen of them, cool and slim and silver-clad.

And every eye was on Tom.

On Tom, who hadn't given the alarm.

Tom took one look at them and forgot all about the demons. He threw himself down from the blackthorn, and he ran.

He didn't stop until he was through the thick belt of trees that encircled the clearing. Then he paused to listen. All quiet. No one following.

He went on again, quietly, slipping along the edge of the wood. In the mist beyond the sickly winter grass was the sprawl of the city of the demons. There were demon outposts all round the woods and scrubby heaths of the common now.

Tom turned across the grass towards an isolated tangle of thornbushes. His nest was there. He wriggled into the lining of wool-snags and curled himself into a ball.

The Tribe had come close to discovery just then. And it had been Tom's fault.

Soon the Tribe would come and sniff him out.

Unless they chose to make him wait.

He waited.

2

The clouds slowly darkened into tender bruises and nothing came near Tom except a chaffinch, which sat and preened itself on a branch above his head. The little bird was winter-thin, nothing but bones and feathers, but —

Tom arranged himself carefully.

One. Two. Three.

Now!

He lunged and grabbed. His sleeve got caught on a bramble, but he managed to catch hold of a handful of needle-sharp claws and suddenly the chaffinch was flapping and fighting for its life. It scratched and pecked and screamed, twisting in his cold fingers. Tom hastily wriggled his other hand up through the branches so he could wring its neck: but it was too late. The bird squirmed and scratched its way to freedom, and Tom was left holding three bloody feathers.

He sucked the blood mournfully off the quills. The hillside was ringing with acid alarm calls now: every creature on the alert. That put an end to any chance of his catching anything — but then there had never been much chance. Tom sighed. No chance of food tonight. Unless he gave himself up to the Tribe.

The winter wind was shrinking his flesh. He shivered and wavered and hugged himself. The Tribe would take revenge on him if he went back — but there was no escape from that, whatever he did. Not in the end.

He huddled back down in his nest. He would wait another hour. Perhaps by then the Tribe would have drunk too deep to care much about him.

Then he would go and give himself up.

Each of the Tribe sat alone, gorging, splashed by the moonlight of the chilly night. Sia, reclining on the grass, was licking a trickle of blood from her arm. She was very, very beautiful, tall and sapling-fine, and she had calved Tom. That was strange, because Tom was slow, and his voice was ugly. Sia had told him so.

A stag lay among the Tribe. Its belly was split from throat to vent and it steamed, new-dead, into the air.

Tom's mouth watered. He slid a foot forward into the moonlight. Every one of the Tribe saw him, but they were feeding and had no time for anything else. Tom sidled cautiously up to the body of the stag. The liver was the lowliest part of the carcass, fit only to be left for the flies — but Tom's teeth were blunt, and he hadn't grown his fangs yet. He drew his knife.

Tom ate, very quiet and still, crouched in the frozen shadow of the stag's body.

The Tribe was pouring glinting streams of scavenged demon wine into their mouths now. Sia's long throat was white above her silver chains. Larn sat a little way away. He was the most skilled hunter in the Tribe, and he was Tom's sire. Larn let the last of the black wine drip into his mouth and threw away the bottle. Tom shrank down even further against the warm flank of the stag.

But the Tribe was full now, and they had attention for him.

"Tom is here," said Sia.

Tom spoke, even though his voice was nasal and thick and they would jeer at him.

"The demons crept up on me," he said; and he was surrounded by cold, high laughter.

"Demons, creeping?" asked a voice, with scorn.

"He must be as blind as a hedgehog."

"He's as hoarse as a hedgehog."

"And deaf."

"And *careless.*"

At that the laughter left them.

"We were nearly discovered," said someone, tall among the long shadows. "That must never happen again."

"He must be taught to stay awake."

"And he must remember."

Tom waited.

Then someone said:

"Give him a prod with a spear."

Tom covered his face with his arms. That was all he could do.

He waited.

The frost creaked as someone came close. Tom made himself as small as he could, but a hand yanked his belt and he instinctively put out his hands as the ground came up at him. But then the ice-toothed grass was spinning dizzily past him and he was swinging, helpless, from his belt. The whole clearing was tumbling and waltzing and his belt was cutting into him — round

7

and round — until he didn't know where he was or what was happening or why everyone was laughing: and then the stars and blackness swept themselves together in a giant swirl and he was flying. Flying.

He landed harder than anything he'd thought possible. For a split second he was aware of several separate things: the sting of a scratch, and the bent-under ankle, and the struggling of his beaten-empty lungs.

But then a larger pain came. It hit him with blaring demon voices and the force of a tidal wave.

His lungs were empty, so he couldn't cry out. The pain rolled over him, and swallowed him, and that was that.

3

Tom opened his eyes to the sky. The first thing he noticed was that the stars looked wrong: small and somehow frozen, so he could hardly make out the bright explosions of their endless battles.

He lay still for a moment, working out where he was. A little way away someone was singing. It was an old song, and the words had been made by demons, but the tune was special to the Tribe.

> *Oh I forbid you, maidens all,*
> *That wear gold in your hair,*
> *To come or go by Carterhaugh*
> *For young Tam Lin is there.*

The Tribe had sweet voices — so pure that sometimes the demon wine bottles would shatter where they lay. It was only Tom whose voice was thick and harsh; only Tom who couldn't sing. He lay among the saw-edges of the frosty grass, listening — remembering. But the song was far away, and it faded as he listened.

Tom pushed himself up. His skull felt full of stones. Slowly, carefully, he pieced together his jagged memories.

He had let demons come upon the Tribe.

And he had paid.

Now that he was sitting up he could hear the song again.

If that I am with child, father,
Myself must bear the blame;
There's not a lord about your hall,
Shall get the bairn's name.

Tom had heard that song many times. It was the story of a Tribe-woman who had taken a demon as her lover — it was unbearable to think about — but had lost the demon in the end to a female of its own kind.

Tom gingerly tried out his arms and legs. They ached horribly, but everything seemed to work.

Tom could catch only a fragment of the next verse.

. . . The queen of Fairies caught me
In yon green hill to dwell . . .

He strained his ears, but as the voice soared it faded
again. Why did it keep fading? Tribe-song was too high
for demons to hear — but now the highest parts of the
song seemed to have vanished for him, too.

The taunting words lurched back at him:

Deaf as well as careless.

Deaf? Was he?

Perhaps his ears had got blocked up. Perhaps he'd
hurt them when he'd hit the ground.

But perhaps —

Perhaps that was why he hadn't heard the demons. It
wasn't that he'd been asleep. He wouldn't have dared to
go to sleep, not out in the open. Perhaps he was going
deaf.

The song would have come to an end by now. The
long, lithe shadows of the Tribe would be going to rest.
And tomorrow demons might come through the common again and Tom might be the nearest to them. But
as long as he kept a really sharp lookout —

He must be as blind as a hedgehog.

11

No. No. Tom squirmed away from the thought. He looked up again at the stars. They studded the velvet of the sky like tiny diamonds — but that was all *wrong*. They should not be so small and bright and dead. They should be consuming the sky with swirling fire.

Suddenly Tom did not trust himself. Where was the Tribe? He thought they had gone to rest, but they might be all around him. If he couldn't see properly, couldn't hear, he was bound to let more demons come. If he brought the Tribe into real danger again —

A blackbird sang a few muted notes to welcome the graying of the sky. Tom pushed himself up wearily and limped his aching bones through the trees towards his nest.

Across the sodden grass a pall of mist softened the city of the demons. Already one or two demon chariots were swooping along their dead roads.

Demons.

If he let demons come again —

Give him a prod with a spear.

Tom thought of the stag, ripped open, steaming.

He couldn't stay. Not with the Tribe. He must go away — except that was hopeless. He could set snares — hope to catch rabbits — but he couldn't keep himself alive like that. Larn could pluck birds from the trees, spear a stag at thirty paces, but wherever Tom went twigs snapped under his feet. They said he made nearly as much noise as a demon.

Demons.

Demons had food. He'd heard tales of it — eaten it, sometimes, after the elders had made a raid on the city.

It was no worse to die from a demon fireball than from a barbed spear that lodged in your flesh.

Was it?

It was morning, but Tom didn't need rest. He had rested all night in the ditch.

Slowly, so he didn't jolt the stones in his head, he began to walk down the slope towards the city of the demons.

4

★ The Tribe did not go lightly into the city of the demons. Demons were stupid, and they were too heavy to move fast, but they were strong enough to snap your bones with their fingers. If one caught you, your only chance was to call upon the stars to make yourself invisible.

Tom made his way down across the grass. The frost had gone except in the shadows of the tussocks, and he left no footprints.

But demons didn't need to get hold of you to kill you: they could shoot bolts of lead that smashed holes right through your body. That was how they killed the deer on the common. The deer leapt, and arched their backs, and fell. Dead. The Tribe's spears were better because they were silent; and they were just as deadly, in the long run.

But then the demons were so strong that they didn't need to be quiet.

Tom came to the edge of the common and there was the demons' road. It was made of harsh, gray stuff that had withered all the plants near it.

Tom stepped onto it.

Tom had never been to the city of the demons before, and it smelled of death. He stood and shivered by the bridge over the river, his skin prickling with danger. It was madness to cross — but then he was in danger if he stayed, too. He slipped across on the shadowy side, ready to call upon the stars to hide him.

On the other side of the bridge was a path made of square stones, and the rows of square clay houses started. Tom walked along carefully, but it was not long after dawn and the demons were still at their morning feasting. There were so many houses it was like looking into a rippled pond — everything reflected, and multiplied, and however often you turned, everything all around you was the same.

And then a little way ahead a door opened. Tom, caught by surprise, pressed himself against a rough clay wall — but the demons who came out were too busy with each other to notice him. They were pressing their lips together. Then the male walked away, but the female and her calf followed it with their eyes until it turned the corner.

Tom nearly vomited. There were slave-ropes that tied that male to the others. Tom could not see them, but he sensed they were there. Ropes that tugged at its mind and forced it to return so the others could feed from it.

Tom backed away, shivering. Suddenly he understood the danger of the demon city. It wasn't being killed: it was being held, and having your mind tied so that you could never be free again. Even Larn was not so cruel as that.

He turned and fled.

5

The houses of the demons were square. Everywhere was the same, relentlessly. Even their plants were fenced and clipped — frost-stiff, sterile, and lonely. Roads ran straight, and crossed, and ran straight again. Tom ran down a path, hesitated, turned a corner, found everything unfamiliar, and stopped.

There were some oak trees a little way away, just beyond those houses. They must be outside the city. Tom turned towards them, but the road he was following bent away. He took a turn, and then another. The sun was coming up fast now, over the mist.

He came to one more corner and almost walked into a great female demon with two calves. One look at her sour face with its gash of scarlet mouth was enough. He jumped up onto a wall where he was half hidden by a straggle of bush and he called upon the stars to take him.

At once the city grew long and blue and Tom felt the lightness of body that told him he had passed from sight. He held his breath as the fat demon and her calves lumbered along past him. The calves were dragging and whining, clopping their feet, but the female held them with hands of leather. They smelled horrible — sharp, and sweet, like the demon wine.

They passed, and Tom took a long, careful breath. He could only manage to stay invisible for a little while, and now that it was broad daylight the roads would soon be full of demons. He had to get out of the city quickly. He stepped off the wall and began to trot down the road.

But the city was even more confusing when it was long and blue, and now that the houses stretched up to the sky he couldn't see that line of oak trees anymore. He kept going, but he soon began to feel the pull of the real world that would make him visible again. He wouldn't be able to resist it for long.

The roads were getting wider and busier now, and there were demons in sight all the time. He turned a corner and suddenly he was on a wide path — and there were so many demons that the whole place stank. He gagged, and turned round to get away — and then the trace of another smell caught him.

Meat.

He stopped, and sniffed again. Yes, over there. A

whole house full of meat. A demon in white was giving some to another demon. There was loads of it, right out in the open, but there were demons walking past and taking no notice. Were they too blind and stupid to see it?

Tom edged closer.

There were bits of sheep arranged on white boards. Tom's mouth watered. He needed food — and there was nothing to stop him from taking some. He would wait until there was a demon standing by the table and then he would reach round and snatch a board.

Here were two demons. Males, not quite full-grown. They were walking quite fast, but Tom could easily nip in behind them and lift a board of sheep from the table.

He did, and it was easy.

For a second.

"Hey!"

The two demons stopped.

"What?"

Tom stuffed the board of sheep up his shirt to hide it and began to edge away.

"Put that back!"

"What?"

"That tray of chops. I saw you. Put it back!"

"He's gone mad."

"Right, I'm calling the police!"

Suddenly it wasn't so easy. All the demons were stopping to look and Tom found himself blocked in by a wrinkled female with a humped back and a bag on wheels. He backed away and managed to slide between a jowly male in a flat cap and a frizz-haired female with a bosom like a log. The demons were blaring away at each other. He was quite near the edge of the crowd now. If he could just get round this vacant-looking one with the bulbous legs he could —

Something hit him violently in the back and he was sprawling on the ground in a tangle of wheels and bag and wrinkly demon before he'd worked out what was happening. The tray of meat shot out of the bottom of his shirt and went visible.

So did he.

"Look!"

"Look at that!"

"Where did he come from?"

"Grab him!"

A hand came down. He ducked, squirmed, crawled, somehow found his feet, and ran.

The paving stones were hard beneath his feet. He

could feel them quivering with the weight of the demons close behind him.

He ran. He took the first turn, and the second, and the third, but all the time he was slow, slow, and they were bound to catch him.

A fourth turn. Square clay houses, and more, and more, and no way out. Perhaps the city was like that. Perhaps there was no way out.

And there really was no way out of this road. It came to an end in a prim semicircle of houses, and that was that. Those demons would turn the corner any moment and —

Hide. There was no time to call on the stars. He had to hide. Anywhere. Over the gate and along the path to a glade where clothes flapped on a line. Quick. Hide. Hide. But where?

Further. Out of sight. Into a bush? Winter. No leaves.

There. At the end of the grass. A hut. Lunge at it with your last breath. Up with the latch. Slide inside with the house windows prickling your skin. Curl on the floor.

Safe.

6

Tom didn't move until he was sure the demons must have given up the search. He didn't move until his heart had gone back into its place and he could breathe properly again.

He sat himself up at last and looked round. The hut was a flimsy thing made of boards. There were tools hung on the wall, a heap of musty boxes and knobbly things, and some strings of onions.

Onions?

Tom checked the window and then helped himself to one.

The onion was so eye-wateringly strong he nearly gave up on it — but it was food, and he crunched his way tearfully all the way through. Then, after a pause to pant some of the fierceness away, he helped himself to another.

Onions were even crunchier than lark bones. The noise filled his head and the strength of them blurred his eyes, and that was why he was so nearly caught. A shadow fell across him from the window and he only had one panic-stricken second to sweep away the onion skins, and another to call on the stars.

The door was opening as he vanished. A huge hand and then a huge foot — fleshy and horrible — and then a bulky shadow that stepped in and resolved itself into a demon. It was stumpy, with thin black hair: a half-grown female.

Then the demon closed the door and Tom was trapped. He pressed himself backwards into a corner and tried not to choke on its smell.

The demon was carrying a whole armful of stuff, and it didn't seem in a hurry. The first thing it did was throw a cushion on the floor and sit down on it.

Then it started talking to itself.

"Well," it blurted out, blaring and coarse and ugly. "I suppose it's better than nothing. It's damp, it's drafty, and it smells of onions, but at least we'll be able to get away from Joe."

As well as the cushion, it had brought a wad of printed paper, a handful of hay, a block of something that smelled rapturously sweet, and half a carrot.

How long is it going to stay? thought Tom in

dismay. Already he could feel himself wavering on the edge of the real world.

The demon reached into its coat pocket and took out something round and shaggy. It was — yes, it was *meat*. Still alive, too. Tom had never seen anything like it — it was like a sort of very scruffy water rat with no tail.

Tom's mouth watered.

The demon was stroking the meat's fur. And it was talking again.

"I'm sorry it's so cold, Sophie," it was saying. "Would you like some carrot?"

The demon settled the meat called a sophie on its lap. The sophie sat and munched at the carrot and the demon stroked its whirls of fur.

If you killed an animal when it was frightened, then its meat turned out tough. Tom supposed the demon was calming the sophie before it wrung its neck.

But the demon didn't seem in any hurry. It stroked the sophie for a while, and then it began to poke around the things it had brought.

Tom had to keep concentrating on staying invisible. The pulling of the real world was very strong now.

The demon began to inspect its wad of paper, very carefully, a sheet at a time, and Tom, nearer and nearer the brink of the real world, wondered if he'd be strong enough to kill the demon if he hit it with a spade.

No chance. Demons were as tough as stone.

But now the demon was moving at last. *Hold on,* thought Tom, gritting his teeth. *Hold on!*

It was getting up and putting the sophie back in its pocket.

"We'd better get back," it said. "At least we've got somewhere to get away from Joe now. Come on, Sophie."

Tom was visible before it'd latched the door. He collapsed, panting, thanking all the stars.

This was no good. He'd only been in the city a couple of hours and twice he'd only just escaped being caught. It was even more dangerous here than on the common. He'd have to go back.

Through the window a sour-looking old demon in the next glade was taking in some clothes.

He waited until it had gone in again. Then he slipped out of the hut and back down the path.

7

Tom didn't even try to remember the way he'd come: he just headed as nearly as he could towards the russet tops of the oak trees, and found himself going downhill. But, of course, the river ran along the edge of the city, so he was bound to have to go downhill. That gave him hope. He turned left, and right, and at last there in front of him was the bridge and the road out to the common.

The common was empty, and quiet, and it was enough just to be away from the square city and its foul-smelling demons. Even the sodden grass was welcoming after the harsh death-trail of the demon road.

He went slowly and quietly, taking comfort in being back where he belonged. He must have been quieter than ever before to come upon Larn unnoticed. Larn was sitting in the broad shoulders of a chestnut tree chipping delicately at a flint.

Tom froze instantly. Larn was unpredictable, and sometimes dangerous. Tom took a quiet step backwards, but a voice from somewhere above him brought him to a halt.

"Larn," it said. "I have words for you."

That was Sia's voice. And she could be dangerous, too. Tom held his breath.

Larn continued chipping translucent flakes of flint.

"What words?"

"Tom is a danger to us."

Larn shifted slightly so that his back was more turned to Sia. That meant he was paying attention.

"He has paid. He will be careful now."

"Care may not be enough. We cannot afford to be seen, Larn. The demons are increasing. Every year they are more. And they are no longer afraid. They are forgetting the tales that have kept them in fear for so long."

"That is true."

Tom stepped carefully, delicately, into the sheltering shadow of a smooth beech-trunk.

"We have always been able to lure away any demon who saw us, even if we did not want it for ourselves," said Sia. "But a clumsy death might bring down a hundred demons upon us."

"That is also true."

When Sia next spoke she seemed to have changed the subject.

"Tom is like Edrin."

There was a pause.

"His voice is the same," agreed Larn.

"He must be dealt with as Edrin was."

Larn gave no answer: but Tom could see his face through the ferny fronds of dead bracken.

He was smiling.

Tom crept away.

8

★ ★ ★ Once, the Tribe had outnumbered the demons: the demons had feared the Tribe then; but that was long ago. Even Tom hardly knew how many of the Tribe lived on the common now, for they were solitary and came together only to feast. Even a female who had calved visited her young only when her breasts were heavy with milk. And once it could crawl it scavenged for itself.

But even so, Tom was almost sure there was no Edrin living on the common. He had approached every female of the Tribe in his time, for sometimes a female would throw food to a calf if she had more than she could eat. But none of them had been called Edrin.

The Tribe did not ask or answer questions, and few of the Tribe remembered Edrin. And those that did, didn't care.

"She is not here," said one, snatching the handful of

late blackberries Tom offered her. "She has not been here for many years."

"Then where is she?" asked Tom.

Her mouth was stained with the dark juice of the blackberries.

"She was a cripple. A danger. Then one day she was not here."

And she crammed the last of the blackberries into her mouth and went off.

Edrin was a cripple. A danger. And then she was not here.

But where did she go?

Tom, who was avoiding the clearing, and particularly avoiding Larn and Sia, went off to check his snares. He was lucky: there was a young rabbit caught in one. It was dead, but not yet frozen.

He ate his first meat in three days, and it tasted good.

There were thousands of demons in the city, but still they grew more. Hardly a year had gone by without more arriving in a new field to scour away the earth to build more houses. It was a belief long held by the Tribe that demons would never build on the common — but they were getting closer all the time.

There were demons all around the common now, littering the countryside and hemming in the Tribe. It was possible to walk along by the hedges of the demon fields northward — but what then? Then there were the duck lakes, and demons hunted there.

Tom kept to his nest, only venturing out to check his snares. He managed, by chewing beechnuts and digging for wild carrot, to keep himself alive; but he was getting thinner and he wouldn't go on like that for long. He could have managed if he'd been completely alone, but the common was full of skilled hunters who took most of the food. It didn't help that his sight was getting worse. Sometimes he would squint up at the stars, trying to make out their flaring splendor. But he couldn't see much more than tiny points of silver: beautiful, but dead.

Tom, alone, never had to speak; but when he stubbed his toe on a tree root, or tore his hand on a rose briar, he found his voice thickening and deepening.

He managed to avoid all sight of Larn and Sia for more than a week, but then one evening he caught the glint of Sia's silver gown through the gloom of the evening trees. He hastily dodged back along a deer path and climbed up through the ivy that clung round the trunk of an ancient beech.

And came face-to-face with Larn.

Tom's first instinct was to drop and run: but Sia was swift and her eyes were keen. They gleamed up at him from the bottom of the tree.

Larn sat in the crook of the tree, at his ease. The Tribe had no leader, but no one was fool enough to dispute with Larn. Tom took a quiet sideways step towards the place where the broken branches of the beech thrust into those of a neighboring ash. Larn sat lazily, not watching, but aware. Then he spoke.

"Stay," he said.

Tom froze with one foot in the air. His heart was suddenly hammering hard.

Larn flicked a glance over him.

"You are afraid," he said mildly.

Tom couldn't think of anything to say. The tree moved a little under him. Sia was climbing up.

They would be able to do anything they liked to him.

Larn yawned, showing his long teeth, as Sia appeared behind him, a silhouette in the dusk.

"Edrin was always afraid," said Sia. "She would whimper and cry and spoil our hunting."

Tom's throat had gone tight: but he made an effort, a huge effort, to speak.

"Who is Edrin?"

Larn answered, still mild.

"Arial, who calved me, calved her also."

Sia hissed.

"She was a cripple. Blind, deaf, useless. She was a danger to the Tribe."

The air around Tom seemed to have grown very thin. His voice came out as a whisper.

"What happened — what happened to her?"

Larn laughed. It was a terrible laugh that flung back his head and needle-edged the shiny ivy leaves with frost. Tom went to step back; but there was nothing behind him.

"He should be told," said Sia.

Larn turned to Tom, and for the first time ever Larn's amber eyes looked into Tom's. They were keen, sharp, beautiful, like the eyes of a fox or an owl.

Hunting eyes.

"I killed her," said Larn.

10

Tom had known — he'd known all the time — but still he couldn't move, couldn't speak. He stood paralyzed in the amber glow of Larn's eyes.

And then somehow he was on the ground. He'd fallen, perhaps. Perhaps. He'd landed, rolled, picked himself up, and was running before he knew he'd moved. Running by instinct, blindly. Running fast.

They were coming after him. He could feel the cold of them. He fled into the dark trees, diving and ducking and twisting. Larn could spear a stag at thirty paces.

Tom threw himself into a great tangle of bushes. He was safe from a spear-throw there, but the going was much slower. The chill of his pursuers was no longer behind him — it was moving round and ahead to cut him off.

He stopped, panic striking at him. If he doubled back he might be able to shake them off, but he wouldn't be safe for long. There was nowhere on the common where he'd be safe for long.

Tom looked up at the sky. He was half starved and very tired — almost too tired — but he summoned up all his strength and called upon the stars to receive him. And they heard him, just, and hauled him away from the world and Tom was left, panting, almost in tears with weakness. He had the strength to stay invisible for only a very few minutes; and in that time he had to get clear away.

But it was hard to move invisible limbs cleanly through the intricate lattice of clutching brambles.

"There!" said Sia. "With your spear. Look!"

"I see him," said Larn.

Tom cast all caution away. He tore himself free of the last of the brambles, and he ran.

Larn's spear scattered the leaves a handsbreadth away but Tom ran on. He ran without thinking into the blue night. He ran and ran until his feet tacked on the demon road — but still there were footsteps behind him.

A small part of his brain was telling him it was best to hide, but there wasn't time to do anything but run.

Even when he reached the bridge and the square clay houses of the city he hadn't time to think.

The city was dark now, looming in long indigo shadows that nearly touched the stars. Tom could feel, stronger and stronger, the pull of the earth that would make him visible again. He had to find somewhere safe; but there was a coldness behind him and inside him and he didn't dare stop.

And here was something new — an open door streaming light into the street. That meant something — but Tom's mind was too jumpy with terror to work it out.

He ran straight on, straight into the light — and straight into something hard.

Tom rebounded, fell, and a massive weight fell on top of him. Tom struggled and squirmed, but he was under something hot and horribly smelly, and he might as well have been trapped under half an oak tree.

The thing yelled as it went down, a blaring demon bellow, and then it lay and swore.

And now more endless cobalt demons were crowding in the doorway. Tom, in a panic, with the stars slipping inexorably from him, gave up trying to push the demon off him and bit its hand instead. The demon snatched back its hand so fast that it nearly took several of Tom's teeth with it.

"What's wrong, Mike?" asked one of the demons.

Mike clutched at its hand.

"It bit me, it bit me!" it screamed. "Get me out of here!"

Tom poked it hard, and it screamed again and rolled away. Tom nearly screamed too, because now all its weight was crushing Tom's ankle into the path.

"Help! Help me up! For God's sake!"

The demons in the doorway looked doubtful, but a couple of them held out their hands. Tom rolled clear and tried to get up, but a colossal wrenching pain in his ankle brought him down at once, nearly tore the stars from his grasp. He gritted his teeth and crawled.

Demon voices followed him up the street.

"What was that all about?"

"He says he got attacked by the Invisible Man."

"*What?*"

"Well, he's got real teeth-marks on his hand, I'll tell you that."

Tom pulled himself up against a wall. He had to get away from here, for he had only a perilous fingernail's grip on the stars now, and the strong pain made him heavy, weighed him down. He tried out his weight on his injured ankle again and found he could just touch his foot down.

He limped agonizingly down the road.

11

The sky was clearing, and there was the promise of a frost in the air.

Tom didn't know where he was going, but at least he seemed to have lost Larn and Sia. Or perhaps they'd left him to be killed by the demons.

He stopped in the shadow of the first dark doorway and let himself fall from the realm of the stars. The relief of that was tremendous. For a moment. But where did he go now?

There was only one place he could think of. It wasn't safe, but it would have to do until he could find somewhere better.

Instinct took him there — to a prim semicircle of clay houses. They were dark, which meant they were safe. He hobbled painfully around the orange smears of the lights that blotted out the stars.

And then, although it was nighttime when every

demon slept, a spear of light sliced the darkness ahead of him.

Tom froze. Something was wrong. There was something awake inside that house. Something had felt him coming and it was searching for him.

But that was impossible. That was a demon house, and no demon had the eyes or wit or knowledge to do anything of the sort.

Tom sidled carefully around the lance of light and up the path of the next house to the fragile safety of the wooden hut.

12

The stars ripped the sky into splendor. Purple, crimson, gold. And then a giant flare exploded hugely across the sky — and Tom ducked, banged his head, and woke up.

The place was filled with pale winter daylight. Tom pushed himself up on one elbow, rubbed his eyes, and fumblingly tried to work out where he was. He was — yes — he was in a demon hut.

And he was staring straight into the startled eyes of a demon.

Its nose was squashed against the glass of the window, dead white.

Tom gaped, tried to think, looked round in panic, tried to think —

It was the young female he'd seen before.

Think!

It'd seen him.

What can I do?

By all the stars, it was coming in!

Stars! The stars! Call on the stars! Quick!

They pulled him out of the world just as the door was opening. The demon peered round the door, first, and then it stepped in. It was so massive it blocked the whole width of the entrance. Tom had managed to get to his feet, but his ankle had seized up in the night and he could hardly put any weight on it at all. There was no hope of barging his way out.

"I know you're here," said the demon. Its blaring voice was wavy at the edges, almost as if it was scared.

Tom held his breath.

"I saw you," said the demon doggedly, its face gray in the light of the realm of the stars. "You were asleep. I saw you. My name's Anna. What's your name?"

The demon stepped forward, swinging its arms to try to find him. Tom pressed himself back into the farthest corner.

"How did you go invisible?" it demanded.

If it came any closer he might just have room to get round it and away.

But it wasn't stupid, and it had decided to search the hut bit by bit. Tom had to duck hastily under a flailing arm — and his ankle couldn't stand it. He had to clutch

43

at the wall to steady himself and in the couple of seconds he was off-balance, the demon's hand touched him. Tom threw himself away, but the demon was surprisingly quick. It lunged forward and flung both its arms round him. Something squeaked.

"Ow!" it exclaimed, letting go for a second and then grabbing again, more carefully, this time. "Sophie? Sorry. Oh, you're so *cold*!"

It was the demon who was hot. Its hands were almost hot enough to burn him.

It was feeling him with heavy hands.

"All right," it said determinedly. "You're wearing clothes, so you're not an animal. And you're not a ghost because I've got hold of you. You're a boy. Or a girl, I suppose. Come visible again!"

The demon was so revolting that Tom couldn't help squirming away from it, but that just made it clutch harder. It was heavier, stronger than anything he'd ever imagined. It felt his sleeve — not roughly — but hard enough to shove him heavily onto his bad foot. The pain was incredible: it was so bad that he nearly passed out.

He lost hold of the stars and tumbled back into the world.

13

"You're real," said the demon wonderingly, gazing right at him. Tom looked away hurriedly; it had googly blue eyes and he could feel it trying to enslave him.

"Let me go," he muttered, through his pain.

"What? What did you say?"

Demons were deaf. He shouted.

"Let me go!"

It considered for a moment and then stepped back. Tom tried to rub its heat away from his arm.

It was still blocking the door.

"Who are you?"

Tom tried for a second to work out a way out of this mess. But it was hopeless.

"Tom."

The demon was a little shorter than he was, but it had great bones worked by heavy muscles and it was rounded off with a thick layer of fat. And it kept looking at him.

"How did you make yourself disappear?"

Tom shook his head. That wasn't the sort of thing you could explain, because it wasn't the sort of thing you could understand: not understand with words, anyway.

"I called on the stars," he said.

It put out a hand and touched him again, and they both winced away again from the difference in their temperatures.

"You can't be dead," it said, but its voice was wavering again. "Not if you can move about. But you can't be *human*."

Tom didn't know what human was.

"What are you?" asked the demon.

Tom opened his mouth and then closed it again. This demon was young and it clearly knew nothing about the Tribe. He heaved a sigh.

"Lost," he said.

14

The demon called Anna closed the door of the hut, took the sophie carefully out of its pocket, and sat down on the floor. Tom sat down too, as gently as he could, keeping his foot clear of the floor. His ankle was still hurting really badly. He laid his cold fingers tenderly round it to protect it from the demon's prying gaze.

"I could bring you a map, if you liked," it said.

"No," said Tom, his face turned away from its stare.

That offended it.

"Well, you shouldn't be hanging round here," said the demon. "It's private property. And you'll die of cold."

Tom didn't *want* to stay: but he didn't know where else he could go.

"Tell me where I can be alone," he said. "Then I will go there."

The demon's eyes seemed to throw out beams of light that searched him through.

"That's not easy," it said. "Especially if you've hurt your foot. Why do you want to be alone? Why can't you go home?"

Tom could feel its great big horrible eyes on him. It was trying to take him over, he could feel it. He swung round on it.

"That is my business," he hissed. "Mine. Keep out!"

Anna's eyes fell. That was good. And it was putting the sophie back in its pocket and heaving itself up.

"Well, this is just what I needed," it said glumly. "Someone else to be nasty to me. I was thinking Joe will be bad enough. It never occurred to me that the shed would be invaded by some sort of ice-cold — *thing!*"

"I am not a thing," said Tom coldly.

Anna stopped with a hand on the latch.

"Then what are you? You aren't human like me, are you?"

He snorted at the thought.

"I am not a demon," he said.

Anna stared — always, Anna stared.

"I'm not a demon!" it exclaimed. "I'm quite nice, really."

Nice? Fat, heavy, puddle-eyed, slow, crow-voiced . . .

"You know," Anna went on slowly. "I know this sounds a bit strange — but could you — could you possibly be some sort of *elf*?"

Tom shrugged. Anna knew something about the Tribe, then, after all.

"Demons have used that word of us," he said shortly.

Anna stared at him until he wanted to hit it.

"I suppose, if you needed to stay here, I could bring you food," it said. "My mum always buys tons of extra stuff when Joe comes. He's my stepbrother: Dad's son."

My stepbrother; *my* mum. Tom's stomach turned with revulsion.

"I suppose you *do* eat?" said Anna.

"Yes," said Tom fiercely. "A lot. As much as I can."

Anna was breathing through heavy lungs.

"And I *was* planning to spend lots of time out here anyway, to get away from Joe."

The sophie began to make small chirruping noises. Tom's mouth watered.

"All right," said Anna suddenly. "You can stay here and I'll help you all I can. But you'd better keep out of everybody's way. You'll have to keep a look out for Edie Mackintosh next door — she's the nosiest person in the world. Mind you, Mum says she's got a heart of gold; but then Mum says that about practically everyone. And then Joe's coming soon. If you see a stringy boy with black hair in the garden you'd better make yourself invisible straight away, because Joe's nasty. Mum and Dad are all right, really: but you know what parents are like."

"Yes," said Tom. "The ones who gave me birth are trying to kill me."

15

Staying in the shed was better than being speared by Larn, but that was all you could say for it. There wasn't room to stretch out, and there was nothing to do. And there was nothing to do, and nothing to do, and the food Anna brought was demon food, bland and square without a scent of blood about it.

Tom limped out to explore the garden that night, once the houses were dark; but the sophie was kept somewhere inside and the back door to the house was locked.

So he made his way back to the shed and chewed his way through a thing Anna had brought him. It was called a bun, and it tasted of rotten wood.

Anna had been right about the next-door demon. It was old, wore a thick coat and a riding helmet tied on with a scarf, and spent hours in its garden shooting suspicious glances all round and poking at things. And when it was inside it was always peering out. That was bad enough, but there was something else about Edie Mackintosh that disturbed Tom. He'd felt it that first night when the light had shone out at him from its house. He'd felt something searching for him — something cold and powerful. He took very great care not to let Edie see him; but Edie had very few chances, because he could hardly walk at all. He only ventured out to drink from the water barrel outside the shed door or to visit the latrine he'd dug round the back. Apart from that he stayed put.

Anna brought him food twice a day. That was good, to feed twice a day — except that Anna kept *talking*, fixing on him with horribly googly eyes and blaring on and on. He gritted his teeth and ignored it as much as he could. Demons talked nonsense, anyway. Anna kept going on about *magic*, but he didn't bother trying to understand. It was all a plot to enslave him. That was why it kept bringing him trinkets — sweet things in colored paper, a cushion, a little folding knife — and that was why it kept asking about his *family* — when they were neither *his* nor *family* at all — and about the common, asking and asking, until the only way to thrust Anna aside was to answer, even though no answer was ever enough to satisfy its endless prying. That was why it kept staring at him, touching him. Demons were demons. And that was easy to remember because Anna was so ugly.

But then, on the third day, feverish, bored, and with an aching ankle, he found himself almost looking forward to Anna's visit.

But, of course, that was only because he was hungry.

Anna still hadn't eaten the sophie, even though it was plainly impossible that the beast could get any fatter. Odd.

Tom's ankle was healing much too slowly, but it was healing. Another day or two and he could move away. He would go — somewhere. Somewhere away from Anna, before he got so used to her — it — that he stopped noticing its blaring heat and blaring voice.

Anna brought him more pale bread that evening, and a blanket. The wool had been spun and woven, or else it would have made a good nest.

"I can't stay," said Anna. "Joe's arrived. He'll be out here nosing about if I'm not careful."

Tom was glad Anna couldn't stay — there was no point in it staying. One more day and he would be gone. Anna would sneak up to the shed — and find it empty. It would carry on leaving out food for him, but he would never come back. And then it would know that it had failed. Failed to enslave him.

"Well — good-bye," said Anna, hesitating in the doorway.

Tom kept his face turned away.

16

✦ Tom put his bad foot down on the ground. Nothing. He stood straight, putting his weight on it. Not a twinge. Good. Tonight he would leave, then. He would travel through the winter night until he found somewhere where there was nobody else. And there he would spend the rest of his life.

A movement outside the window caught his eye — but it was only Anna, plodding across the drenched grass. She was clutching something under her heavy coat.

"Hey! Anna!"

That was a new voice. Tom dropped down out of sight.

"What?" demanded Anna.

"What have you got under your coat?"

"Get lost."

There were heavy footsteps, getting closer. And then there was a scuffle, and then a squawk.

"Sweet rolls," said the new voice, with relish. That must be Joe. "You wait till I tell Evelyn. I bet they were bought specially for tonight."

"Give them back!"

And then there was another scuffle, which ended in a howl of anguish.

"You vicious little *rat*! You wait till I show Dad what you've done. I'm bleeding!"

"Serves you right."

"No wonder you're so fat."

"I'm not fat!"

"I bet you go up to the shed and stuff yourself every day. Four rolls. No one else could eat four whole rolls."

"They're not for —"

Anna bit off her words too late. Tom cursed.

"Not for you?" Joe was suddenly interested. "Who are they for, then?"

Pause.

"Have you got a pet in there?"

"No."

"Liar!"

"I'm not a liar."

"We'll soon see about that."

"No! Don't you dare! That's *my* shed!"

"Let go of me. Get out of the way."

They were coming in. Tom pressed himself against the far wall of the shed and tried to banish all feelings of feverishness. He took a deep breath and he called on the stars with all his strength.

And he waited.

17

"See?" said Anna, with just a hint of relief.

The new demon — Joe — was gangling, near full height, with a bony, star-shadowed face. It was stringy, too, for a demon.

It scowled around the shed.

"I bet it's some sort of vermin. Nothing else would stay anywhere near you. I bet it's a rat."

"An invisible rat," said Anna, sarcastic.

Anna was so stupid Tom wanted to strangle it. The more Anna annoyed this demon, the more determined it would be to find out Anna's secret. It was glaring around. Its hard eyes were pale — almost like the eyes of one of the Tribe. Tom flinched as they passed over him.

"Where have you got it hidden?"

If Anna would only walk away this other demon would follow. But Anna was too stupid to realize that.

"I've already got a pet," she said. "I've got Sophie. Have you still got your hamster, Joe?"

Joe hissed contemptuously and got down so it could look under the jumble of things in the corner. Then it hissed again, and got reluctantly to its feet.

"You must be crazy bringing food out to the shed for things that aren't here. I'll tell Dad, and he'll have you locked up."

"No he wouldn't."

"That's where you *should* be. In a loony bin."

The demon brought its hands up in front of its face, gibbering, and making small hooting noises.

"Totally bonkers," it said. "No wonder Dad said he was fed up with you."

Anna's face went bright red.

"You *liar*!"

Demons were so stupid. If they hated each other they should leave each other alone. It was almost as if they *enjoyed* hating each other.

Joe was enjoying it, anyway: it backed away from Anna in pretend terror and Tom had to squeeze himself even farther into the corner.

"Ooh, ooh! Be careful, Anna! Don't hurt me, don't hurt me — *ouch*!"

Tom doubled up with a gasp, but that was covered up by Joe's yelp of anguish. Anna's hand flew up to its

59

mouth, but luckily Joe wasn't bothering about Anna. It was cradling its elbow tenderly.

"Now look what you made me do!" it snapped. "You've made me smash my elbow on the —"

It glanced round, broke off, and stared, affronted, at the empty space behind it. Tom pressed his hand against his head where Joe's elbow had hit him and took a sideways step.

"You can have half of the sweet rolls," said Anna, suddenly.

Joe swung round, even more suspicious, and just brushed the front of Tom's tunic with its hand. Tom froze.

So did Joe. The demon turned back, and very gingerly pushed out its hand. Tom dropped down to the floor, but there just wasn't room. His knee hit a pile of plastic flower pots. They swayed, balanced breathtakingly, then tipped and bounced and clattered down onto the wooden floor. Joe made a blind grab and caught Tom by the shoulder.

Tom twisted and pulled and got free quite easily. He dived over to the far corner of the shed and kept absolutely still.

Joe stared round him, cursing.

"What's the matter?" asked Anna.

"There's something in here," said Joe, exasperated. "Something big and alive."

"I can't see anything," said Anna. "What sort of thing is it?"

Joe scowled at her.

"At a guess I'd say it was the sort of thing that eats sweet rolls," it said. It began to sweep its hands round, searching, just as Anna had done. It would get him in a moment and Tom could only think of one thing to do.

He waited for his chance, grabbed, and bit all in the same movement. Joe yelled and snatched back its hand, staring in horror at the blood spouting from its finger. Tom didn't wait. He ducked under Joe's elbow and made for the door.

He would have got clear away if Anna hadn't stepped forward suddenly. Tom charged straight into her and that gave Joe a moment to recover. Joe lunged out into the air and found a face, an arm. Tom wriggled desperately, but Joe got him round the neck. Tom kicked back and connected with something: Joe swore, but didn't let go. It tightened its grip until Tom could hardly breathe.

"Don't!" said Anna shrilly. "Let him go!"

The huge weight of Joe's strong muscles were pressing round his neck. It was hopeless. Tom stopped struggling.

"What is it?" demanded Joe.

"Let him *go*!"

"Tell me what it is or I'll break its neck."

The arm tightened even more and a mist came up before Tom's eyes. What air he could draw in smelled suffocatingly of demon.

"He's . . . a boy," said Anna reluctantly.

A hand felt down Tom's arm to his hand and then away again.

"How come he's invisible?"

Anna was tying her fingers in knots.

"I don't know. He's not — I don't think he's human."

"What?"

The arm round Tom's neck relaxed for a second. Tom twisted and ducked, but the arm jerked tight again and nearly wrenched his head off.

"Keep *still*! Have you ever seen him?"

"Well — yes."

"All right, you. *I* want to see you! Make yourself visible!"

Tom couldn't have hung on much longer in any case. He let himself fall back from the realm of the stars.

18

"Now let him go," said Anna.

Joe couldn't do it fast enough. Joe stepped away hastily and stared. Always, demons stared.

"Where did he *come* from?" asked Joe. It was so amazed that for the first time it didn't sound fierce.

"I found him in the shed."

"He's pale, isn't he? Practically white."

"He's one of the Tribe," explained Anna. "They live on the common. They always have, he says, for hundreds of years. So I think —"

"What?"

Anna looked embarrassed, and a bit defiant.

"I think he's some sort of — elf-thing."

Joe opened its mouth to say something, but then changed its mind.

"Can he talk?"

"Yes."

Joe poked Tom in the chest.

"How did you make yourself invisible?" it demanded.

Tom wished he were strong enough to kill Joe.

"The stars took me," he said shortly.

Joe let out a yelp of amazement and derision.

"He sounds like a chipmunk!"

"Don't be horrible."

Joe took no notice. It was thinking.

"What do you mean, the stars took you?" it demanded.

Anna was struggling to open the package of rolls.

"You'd better come away from the window, both of you, or we'll have Edie nosing round."

That made sense. Tom dropped down in a corner and Joe folded its great legs awkwardly into the small space that was left.

"It's impossible, anyway," it said irritably. "The science, I mean — of being invisible — I mean, it's impossible."

Anna handed Tom and Joe a roll each. It was bland and cold, but the white mucus on top was sweeter even than honey.

"You'd be right up there with Einstein and Newton

and Hawking if you could do invisibility," went on Joe. "Just think of it."

Anna looked wistfully at the two remaining rolls, sighed, and tucked them into the watering can for safety. "We'd better save those," she said. "I don't know if I'll get a chance to come out again today."

"What's he doing in here?" asked Joe suddenly.

"He's hiding from his parents. They're trying to kill him," said Anna. "They've already killed his Aunt Edrin."

"Why?"

Tom hated all this. These demons kept on looking, and talking, trying to get inside his brain so they could take him over. He hated them.

"Leave me alone!" he said fiercely. "I do not need you. I do not want you. It is all my business, not yours."

Anna's eyes were on him again, big and round and tragic. Suddenly, sickeningly, he felt the pain he had caused her — not just knew it, but felt it. *Felt* someone else's thoughts. That meant she was very close to en-slaving him: and that made him hate her even more.

"You do need me," she said bravely. "You need me to bring you food."

"Not now. Not now that I can walk again. I do not need demons, I do not need anybody."

Joe grunted with grudging respect.

"That's how I'm going to be, as soon as I'm sixteen," he said.

"Oh, yes," said Anna rudely. "I can just see you living by yourself. You couldn't even find your shoes this morning."

"Don't be pathetic. No," his voice got quieter, less blaring. "I'm going to be a scientist. All by myself. No family. Just facts."

That was so important that Tom had to speak, even though it was to a demon.

"Where is the place where you can live alone?"

Joe gave him a sharp look. Then he sat back and regarded Tom nastily.

"So," he said, with more than a hint of triumph. "You're here because you haven't got anywhere else to go."

Tom didn't say anything.

Joe laughed. It wasn't a nice laugh; it reminded Tom of Larn.

"I think you do need our help, after all," it said.

19

"You're outnumbered, you know that," said Joe.

All demons tried to enslave everyone they came across; but they were cunning and did it in different ways. Anna's way was with nosiness, and presents, and sheer heavy persistence; and Joe's was with fear — but that was easy to ignore. If the things Joe was saying hadn't been so vitally important Tom wouldn't even have bothered to listen.

"There are millions of us demons," Joe was saying, with horrible relish. "Millions and millions of us, all over the place. Every day loads more demons arrive and build more houses. There's hardly anywhere in the whole country now where you're not in sight of a demon house."

Anna was listening. She was stupid, but she wasn't a coward; and she would have said if Joe were telling lies.

"And demons are really horrible," Joe went on. "You're lucky you were found by Anna, because she's too small and stupid to do anything much to you; but most demons are really cruel and wicked."

"No we're not," said Anna. "Not everyone is as horrible as you. Everybody else is quite nice, most of the time. Except for Mrs. Hitchen, at school, of course."

Joe hissed contemptuously.

"You don't know anything."

"Yes I do. And we're not half as bad as Tom's Tribe. We don't go around killing our children, do we?"

"Oh, yes, we do. It's in the paper all the time."

"That's just the newspapers."

"No, it's not. What about Dad? He's practically abandoned me."

"No, he —"

"And now Mum's gone off."

"But that's only for a few weeks!"

"And that's only some of the wicked, evil things demons do," said Joe, leaning so close that Tom could feel hot demon breath on his face. "That's what we do to our own kind. So you can hardly imagine what we do to other species. Then we *really* have some fun. We shut birds in tiny cages so they can't stretch their wings; and when that drives them mad, we stop them from killing each other by cutting off their beaks."

"Don't!" said Anna, putting her fingers to her ears.

"And we do much worse things than that. When we find a new creature like you, we take it apart to find out how it works. Strip off its skin. That's the first thing, so we can get at the insides."

"If you *touch* him I'll tell Dad!" said Anna.

Joe shook his head.

"If Dad finds out about Tom, he's dead. Dad'd tell the police. Wouldn't he?"

"Well," said Anna doubtfully. "I suppose —"

"And the police would hand him over to the scientists. And *they*'d take him right to pieces. Slice his eyeballs and pull out his fingernails. Would you like that, Tom? Because the only person who can save you — is me."

Tom hated Joe so much he felt as if he had a silver knife in his heart. He was so choked with it he couldn't speak.

"And you'd never get away from here without being caught," Joe whispered. "There are millions of demons for a hundred miles all around. But I could get you away. I could get Dad to take you somewhere miles from anywhere. If you were invisible we could take you in the car and no one would know."

69

It was the faintest straw of hope, but Tom clutched at it.

"When could you take me?" he asked.

Joe sat back and grinned a nasty satisfied smile.

"When I'm ready," it said. "I want to find out about being invisible first."

20

Demons took pleasure in prying, in dissecting, in the laying open of souls: they were evil and cruel.

And some were even worse than others.

"We'll need to measure you first," announced Joe. "Have everything scientific. Anna, go and get a tape measure. And a thermometer."

Anna wavered a little.

"I don't see why you shouldn't get them yourself," she said.

"Do you want me to tell Dad?"

Anna hung around for a little while longer, but Joe turned its face away from her and in the end she let herself out of the shed and ran off down the cold path.

Tom knelt on the floor hating Joe with all his soul. Now that they were alone, Joe might do anything. Joe was clever: clever enough to be really inventive.

"Go invisible!" commanded Joe.

Tom had shaken his head before he thought about it.

"There is no need," he said.

"Yes, there is. I want to see if it happens gradually or all at once. And I want to see if you change color first, or glow, or anything. Or if there's a smell."

Tom shook his head again.

"It is not a thing for play," he said. "It is important."

Joe laughed mockingly.

"Oh yes, it's important," it said softly. "Because unless you cooperate there's no point in me helping you, is there? I might as well call the scientists straight away. Perhaps I should, anyway. They'd be able to make a map of your DNA. Wouldn't that be interesting? They say humans share ninety-eight percent of our genes with chimpanzees. I wonder how many we share with you?"

Perhaps if he became invisible he could throttle Joe. Throttle Joe until its eyes popped out and its face went blue. . . .

"I'm waiting," said Joe.

Tom gave up. He lifted up his hands and called on the stars.

21

"Wow!" said Joe, staring at nothing.

Tom moved stealthily a step to the left so Joe was gaping over his shoulder. He felt much better then. He flicked a glance at Joe. Joe had turned long and blue; and Tom realized, with a tingling shock, that now Joe could almost be one of the Tribe. The blueness had taken all the color from his face, and his new height had stretched him so he was almost graceful.

And his face was like a skull.

They both shivered a little.

"That was *incredible*," Joe said. "There wasn't a flash or anything. You just — went. Where are you now?"

Tom didn't answer. He stealthily picked up a nail someone had left on the windowsill. Then when Joe was looking the other way he chucked it at the door.

Joe whipped round. "Oh, no, you don't!" he muttered, and flung himself on the space by the door. He only managed to stop himself from falling over by do-ing a complicated sort of tangled dance — and even then he hit his arm on the wall. Joe turned round again, scowling viciously.

"What did you do that for? Where are you?" He pushed out his hand — but he must have noticed the teeth marks on his finger because he snatched it back rather hastily. "All right," he said. "You fooled me: what did you do? Throw something? You can come visible now."

Joe was scared. Tom stood there, triumphant, and enjoyed it. When he was invisible he was the stronger one. He would have to remember that. Demons had al-ways feared the Tribe. Demons were afraid of many things — of the dark, of the dead.

Heavy footsteps pounded the grass outside and Anna pushed open the door.

"I got —" Then she stopped and looked around. "Where's Tom?"

"Invisible," said Joe sourly.

Anna dug into her pocket and took out a small glass tube.

"Here we are. Tom, this is a thermometer. It doesn't

hurt, it just measures how hot you are inside. You have to put this end under your tongue for a minute. Here, you'll have to take it and do it yourself, because I can't see you."

Tom hesitated; but then, curious, he took the fragile tube from Anna.

"Wow," said Joe, again. "It's vanished. But then I suppose it would. I mean, his clothes vanish with him, don't they?"

"It's a good thing he *can* vanish," said Anna. "I was stopped by Edie Mackintosh just now."

"Silly old bat," said Joe dismissively. "Why does she always wear that stupid riding helmet? I bet she's bald."

"No, she's not. And she was asking all sorts of questions. What we were doing in the shed and stuff."

Tom put the thermometer cautiously under his tongue. It was uncomfortable, and it tasted faintly metallic. He waited for something to happen.

"What did you tell her?" demanded Joe. "That you were playing mummies and daddies with your nice brother?"

Anna shook her head.

"She's clever. She wouldn't have believed it."

"That old bat!"

"I think — I'm pretty sure she knows we've got someone in here."

Tom remembered the shaft of light that had discovered him, pierced him, the night he'd arrived. Had that been Edie Mackintosh?

Suddenly the dangers Joe had threatened him with seemed very near and very real. Joe was right, curse him. Tom did need them.

Tom took the thermometer out of his mouth and let himself come back into the real world. The thermometer didn't seem to have done anything. Joe snatched it, turning it and squinting.

"I can't find the mercury," he complained.

"Let me see," said Anna, without hope.

"You're supposed to get a bar of silver that tells you the temperature. But I can't see anything."

Anna stood on tiptoe behind Joe and tried to see from there.

Suddenly she made a little noise between a word and a gasp.

"What's that?" she asked. "On the part he's had in his mouth?"

Joe gave it half a glance. Then he looked again, more

carefully. Very gently he touched the fringe of white that had formed round the bulb at the end of the thermometer.

He looked up, half in wonder, half afraid.

"Frost," he said.

22

It was certain that Edie Mackintosh suspected something. No one would spend so much time in a garden otherwise. Not, especially, in winter, when there was hardly anything out there to eat. Edie Mackintosh was in the garden now in her silly helmet and bulky coat, poking about with a hoe. It was a particular nuisance because Tom needed to visit his latrine.

"Joseph! Joseph!"

Tom peered cautiously over the windowsill. Joe had been caught.

"Going out to the shed again, are you?"

"No," said Joe. "I'm emigrating to Australia."

Edie Mackintosh peered suspiciously at him under the brim of her helmet. "Is your sister coming out as well?"

"Half-sister," he corrected her coldly.

"What?"

"Anna. She's not my sister. She's my half-sister."

Edie narrowed her eyes.

"I'm surprised a great lad like you would want to play with a little girl like Anna," she said.

Joe looked murderous — sometimes he was very like one of the Tribe — but he didn't do anything to her. But then Edie Mackintosh was an easy person to hate: she had a sharp voice, and sharp eyes, and a sharp nose, and inside her stupid clothes she seemed to be not much more than a skeleton. And she knew something.

Tom heard someone open the back door.

"Here comes your dad," announced Edie Mackintosh. "Bernard!"

Bernard was huge — broad, and hot with fat. He had black-sheep hair, fuzzy eyebrows that met over his nose, and a heavy mouth that was always falling open.

"Morning, Edie," he said, and tried to walk on; but Edie wasn't letting him get away.

"Isn't it nice for you to have Joe here for once?"

Bernard made a strangled noise and stopped.

"It's not so often that he comes, is it?"

"Just when Mum has to go away on business," said Joe maliciously.

Bernard made a harsh sound in his throat.

"But it's great to have him here," he said, rather brusque. "Really great," he amended, trying to make up for his brusqueness.

"And what's Joe been up to while he's been visiting?"

"He doesn't know," said Joe. "He's been at work the whole time."

Bernard was swaying from side to side like a tethered bull.

"I have to go to work, Joe," he said.

"Oh, I know. I mean, you wouldn't want to waste any days off on me, would you?"

Bernard opened his mouth to say something and then changed his mind.

"I'll be here on Saturday and Sunday," he said, at last, suddenly quite mild. "Perhaps we could do something then."

Joe snorted, and walked off.

Edie watched him go.

"It must be hard for a child when he's from a broken home, mustn't it?" she said.

Bernard snorted and walked off too.

23

The days were short now, and wild. Although there had been no frost for a week, the shed seemed to be getting increasingly cold and uncomfortable. Tom asked Joe when Bernard would be able to take him away.

"A few more days," said Joe. "I've been nagging him to take some time off work, which he's not allowed; so he can hardly refuse to do something with me on Saturday."

Tom shuddered. Demons made slaves of each other all the time — but it seemed terrible to boast about it.

"Look," Joe went on, "here's Dad's old chemistry set. Spit on this litmus paper, and then you can do it again when you're invisible."

Tom shook his head.

"Not now," he said.

Joe jutted out his jaw.

"Look —"

"No," said Tom again. "It is — I don't know. I think I am not well."

Joe snorted.

"There's nothing wrong with you!"

But there was. Tom didn't know what was wrong, but he felt restless and dissatisfied and *hot*. That was the thing. But it was confusing, because he felt cold, too, at the same time.

"Hmm," said Joe. "Perhaps it's the food. You're used to eating mostly meat, aren't you? And Anna's been feeding you sweet rolls."

Anna had also brought him a coat. It smelled strongly of demon sweat, but in the long chill of last night he'd been very glad to have it.

"Let me see you *try* to go invisible," said Joe.

"I can't," said Tom.

"Try," said Joe. Tom looked at him; at his sallow face with its staring gooseberry eyes, and his heavy sinewy arms. Tom felt a fresh surge of hatred because even now Joe was trying to enslave him. Joe was sending out invisible creepers that were reaching for his soul. Tom shuddered uncontrollably.

Joe took hold of Tom's arm. His fingers were heavy; strong enough to crush Tom's bones.

"Try to go invisible," Joe said menacingly.

Tom nearly tried it; but he just knew he mustn't. Something was happening to him inside, and he knew he wouldn't be able to reach the realm of the stars. If he tried, something dreadful would happen.

Joe put his head down and breathed foul fumes in Tom's face.

"You're not going to try to go back on our bargain, are you?" he asked, quite quietly. "Because I can easily call the police, if that's what you want."

"No," said Tom, hating harder than he'd ever hated before.

"Then call on your stars, you little runt."

Tom tried to snatch his arm away — but Joe was four times stronger than he was.

"Perhaps it would be easier with a broken arm," suggested Joe evenly.

"No!" said Tom. He'd never be able to fend for himself if his arm was broken. He'd die of starvation like Linna had done last year. And Joe could break his arm quite easily. Tom tried to think: but Anna had gone out into the city to get food, and there was no way out.

There was a hammering inside his head, but that

was mostly the force of his hatred. Perhaps it was that that was making him feel so ill.

"I'll count to five," said Joe. "One, two —"

There was no way out. Despairing, Tom reached for the stars.

24

It was too far. He'd known it would be. He tried to kick himself upwards, but there was no strength in him, and the realm of the stars remained far ahead — far, far out of reach.

And he was falling — back through infinities of darkness. That was all right — cool and easy — until he reached the edge of the air that encircled the earth. He hit it hard and suddenly everything was hot, scorching hot. There were flames in his eyes, on his hair, in his lungs. He clutched himself into a ball and he screamed; and through the noise, somewhere, someone else was screaming too.

Then he was still. Still, in the outside air, crouched and shivering. He couldn't remember what had happened, but he was shaking all through and he knew that something was disastrously wrong.

He made himself open his eyes. Everything was

black, charred and black. There was smoke rising up around him from planks of smoldering wood.

A little way away, something was bellowing. A demon. Bellowing.

The smoke dodged and twisted and Tom found himself staring at a wall. And more than a wall, a house — a square clay house such as demons built.

"*Joe!*"

A new voice, clear and high, but demon for all that.

"Oh my God. *Joe!*"

The bellowing turned into a howl.

"What happened? Are you all right? *Oh my God, what have you done to the shed?*"

Tom moved. He didn't know what was happening, but the shed was gone and he was hidden only by the wreathing smoke. He crawled to the edge of the garden and slid his way down through the stick-like remains of past-summer's flowers to the passageway between the houses.

There were no windows in the sides of the houses, but there were doors. Tom's scalp prickled with special danger, but he was too confused to know where the danger was.

It was in the next-door house. A bony hand shot out of the doorway and caught hold of him.

"What *did* you do to the shed?" someone asked.

25

Edie Mackintosh was thin, for a demon, but she was strong. Tom struggled, but he was too weak and dizzy for it to do any good.

"Stop that!" said Edie Mackintosh. "You come in here with me."

The demon doorway was hollow with danger. A blast of heat came out at him — heat like only summer brought — and with it a smell of honey and old vegetables and menace.

He thought of biting her; but somehow he didn't.

And then the house had closed round him, all walls and doors and bitty things that lurked in the gloom. The windows had cobwebby sheets hung over them and everywhere was blindingly hot. Edie Mackintosh pulled him through the dimness to a place where a cage of red-hot bars pulsed out scorching heat and everything was dusty and stuffed. She pushed him at one of the stuffed things. It was so stuffed he didn't hurt himself when he fell into it.

"Now you stay there," snapped Edie Mackintosh. "And don't touch anything!"

She was only gone for a minute. Tom sat and tried to think; but the fire was beating on him and it was melting his mind. He knew that something had happened in the realm of the stars, but —

Edie Mackintosh came back with a gray bowl and an armful of cloths.

"Let's see what damage you've done to yourself," she said. And she lunged at him.

Tom ducked, but she caught him in the face. The cloth was wet and squelchy. It left him breathless, but at least the cold of it cleared his mind. And he realized what was happening.

A demon. He'd been caught by a demon. He was in a demon house with the terrible Edie Mackintosh and —

"Filthy," said Edie Mackintosh. "Look at the dirt on this towel! Still, that's only a little cut."

The towel was streaked with ashes and blood. How had he come to be in a fire? He couldn't remember. The last thing he remembered was being in the shed. With Joe. That was it. And he remembered Joe screaming.

"So what's your name?" demanded Edie Mackintosh.

He sounds like a chipmunk.

Tom shook his head. His voice would give him away at once. And anyway, the heat was making him feel very ill: his heart was hammering so hard that it was difficult to breathe.

"You might as well tell me," said Edie Mackintosh. "You've got a lot to answer for. That's a felony, that is, blowing up other people's sheds."

The shed. Yes, he remembered the shed. But then he also remembered sitting inside a circle of charred planks like a huge burst barrel — and he had a horrible feeling that was the shed as well.

"I'll have to phone Social Services," said Edie Mackintosh. "Or the police."

The police. What had Joe said? It was the police who took you to the scientists to be taken apart.

"Well?" demanded Edie Mackintosh. "Have you lost your tongue?"

Tom was sure that if his mind had been clear he could have found his way out of all this. But he was still dazed from — whatever had happened — and on top of that, and the heat, there was something else in this house that was making him feel even worse.

"It's not as if you can go anywhere in that state," Edie Mackintosh said. "Not with half your clothes burned off. And it wouldn't be safe with the shock that you've had. I think I'd better phone Social Services and see what they say."

She went out of the room and talked to someone who couldn't really have been there, because at the end of the one-sided conversation Edie Mackintosh said: "Yes. I'd be glad if you could come round. Thank you. Good-bye."

Then she came back, gave him a penetrating glare, and turned up the fire.

And then she sat down and watched him.

26

The heat was like water. It swam over you so you could hardly see, hardly hear, and then it cast you up in a strange world.

And now through the rusty mist there was another demon roaring.

It had a flaccid bloodred mouth and mildewy hair. It was poking its powdery face at him.

"Don't you feel able to tell me your name?"

The heat caught the sound and mushroomed it.

"It's no good," said Edie Mackintosh, very close but somehow also very far away. "He won't speak."

The powdered face receded a little.

"It's strange that I don't know him. Either his family's new to the district or he's a runaway: but there's no one of his description on the list." It lunged its head forward again, fish-eyes bulging. "I want to help you," it bellowed.

Tom stayed very still and tried not to breathe in its smell.

"Perhaps he's from a family you've not come across," suggested Edie Mackintosh.

"Not likely. He's clearly very disadvantaged. I mean, he's wearing odd shoes, and he's either mute, or very disturbed. And he smells as if he's been making some sort of fire: we get that quite a lot, in winter, with displaced children."

"Oh, the neighbors have been having a bit of a fire out the back. How long do you think it'll be before you trace him?"

"Shouldn't be long. His school's bound to report him missing, even if his family doesn't."

"And until then?"

"Oh, we'll take him into care."

The demon poked out a hand. It had long claws painted to match its lips.

"I'm here to take care of you," it bellowed, showing its teeth.

Edie Mackintosh made a tut-tutting noise.

"The boy's scared out of his wits," she said. "Goodness knows what he'll make of Laidlaw House. I suppose that's where you'll be taking him."

"Oh, they're very experienced —"

"Experienced is the word. No, I think you'd better leave him with me."

The other demon's mouth twitched scornfully.

"I'm afraid we don't just leave children with —"

"Of course you don't. Regulations stacked as high as the ceiling. I should know — twenty-eight children I've had pass through this house from Social Services, not counting my own. You're new to the district, aren't you?"

"Oh. I see. And you'd be willing —? Well, I'll have to put it all through the office, but —"

The heat was as thick as honey. Tom desperately needed to say something, or do something — but anything he said or did would lead to certain disaster.

He was going to be left with Edie Mackintosh, who knew things, who was dangerous.

But then every demon was dangerous. And he felt so ill.

He sat, trying to struggle his mind into thinking, while the demons talked.

27

Edie Mackintosh gave him meat. He stuffed it in his mouth as soon as he possibly could, and nearly went mad with greed while he was waiting, but even so she complained that he let it get cold. He ate it all, every scrap, scorched as it was, even the puddles of meat-tasting slime that it sat in. It must have done him good, because after that the heat of the house seemed a little less unbearable; although he still felt as though he was falling, very softly and slowly, down an end-less well.

Edie Mackintosh took him up to a night-room after he'd eaten. She stood at the door, and for a moment he thought she was going to come in after him: that she would touch him, twist tight demon bonds around him, smother the life out of him in the way of her demon kind. But he bared his teeth at her; and she made a noise between a sigh and a snort and went away.

The room contained a huge cloth-draped thing that you were supposed to sleep on; but he hardly slept at all, because when he wasn't being irritated by the itchy powderiness of the soot that was ground into his skin, or the heat, then the darkness itself lured him awake. At least the heat shut itself down at midnight, which was something; but it was then that he finally worked out what else was disturbing him about the house. Outside every window and doorway in the house was hung a hoop of mossy alder twigs. They were just horrible: they jangled out shrill vibrations that set his teeth on edge and quivered his brain and body into something like jelly. He hated them — when he went close they sent every nerve in his body shrieking.

He ended up lying on the floor as far as he could get from the window, trying to ignore the endless jangling. There was little chance of rest; just hours and hours to realize just how much danger he was in.

Edie Mackintosh knew more about him than any demon should. That had been plain for some time; and, to make things even plainer, she had charms of alder twigs to prevent any member of the Tribe getting into her house.

There were two things he needed very much to know.

Firstly, why did Edie feel herself under threat from the Tribe?

And, secondly, with all the exits guarded, however was he going to get out?

28

The next morning, Tom woke up from a scanty sleep to find the house not quite so hot; but that was probably part of his illness, because he also felt even further from the stars than he had yesterday. Even further from himself, too, in some way he didn't understand.

And the shed. There was nothing left of the shed except a charred square in next-door's garden. From his bedroom window, Tom watched Joe grimly loading all the black and twisted remains into a wheelbarrow and stacking them up by the fence. Three tree-scrambling demon calves had watched Joe, too, sniggering, until Joe had shouted foul things at them and threatened them with a sooty plank.

Bernard lumbered out to watch the last of it.

"Not much left," he said heavily. "Pity about all my tools."

"I said I was sorry!"

"I know, I know. But you need to know what you're

doing, Joe, before you start messing about with weed-killers and chemicals and such stuff. If you're interested in that sort of thing perhaps we could go to the Science Museum some time."

"I've been," snarled Joe.

The next morning, too, saw the arrival of another demon into Edie Mackintosh's house. This was a full-grown male, but it was past its prime. It was soft and plump, with a shiny face and sparse hair and a smile that hid its thoughts.

This new demon also asked questions — but that was no problem, because Tom didn't answer any of them. No voice, no past: and don't let any demon near because Tom was too cold to be one of them.

The demon didn't get flustered or annoyed. It sat, smiling inoffensively, waiting for answers. That meant he was there rather a long time.

"I suppose he's seen a doctor?" asked the demon, at last.

"Not yet, no," said Edie Mackintosh. "I'd made an appointment for this morning, but as you were coming —"

"Oh, I see. Well, he'll have to have a thorough checkup, of course. He's rather pale — from what I can see of him through all that dirt. He might have hearing problems. Or it might just be that he can't understand English."

"Oh, no, he understands every word you say. He's just being stubborn."

The demon smiled his thought-hiding smile.

"Well, there must be some good reason, if he is. Isn't there . . . er —" he stopped, and smiled yet again. "I do wish I knew your name," he said.

"I've decided to call him Tom," said Edie Mackintosh, and watched Tom flinch as the name passed over him. How did she know that? What had she heard when he'd been in the shed?

"Did he tell you his name?" asked the demon quickly.

Edie shook her head.

"I told you, he hasn't said anything," she said. "But he looks like a Tom. And you can see he answers to it."

"Right," said the demon. "Well, I'll be interested to see the results of his checkup." He looked at his watch. "Right. Well, good-bye . . . er . . . is it all right to call you Tom?"

Don't answer.

The demon smiled.

"Do you *dislike* being called Tom?"

Don't answer.

"Well, good-bye, anyway."

Edie Mackintosh was showing him out, talking on about nothing, the weather, nothing, nothing, nothing. And then the door closed and the demon was gone.

Edie Mackintosh came back into the front room. She was rubbing her arms irritably.

"I think it's colder in here than it is outside," she complained. "I keep having to turn the heat up. It's as if something was leaching all the heat out of the house."

Tom sat without moving, but his heart did the thing it did when he accidentally stepped into a rabbit hole. Edie stood a little way away and even without looking at her he could tell that her stare was accusing and suspicious.

"You'll have to talk sometime," she said. "Joe may have taken all the blame for the shed, but you're lucky no one called the police over that — it's taken this long for Mrs. Hodges's cat to come home. You're just making trouble for yourself, Tom."

And then, as he still didn't turn to look at her, she said:

"After all, how close an examination do you want the doctors to give you?"

And then she turned and walked out.

29

Tom discovered that day that the house had a latrine pool-thing that swallowed everything up in a great slurp of rushing water. That was a good thing, on the whole, because Edie Mackintosh had hung sprigs of rosemary on all the alder wreaths and made it even more impossible for Tom to pass them. There wasn't much point in going outside, anyway, because outside there was the Tribe, and a multitude of demons, all of them out to get him. In here there was only Edie Mackintosh — though what she wanted with him was anybody's guess. Edie Mackintosh stared at him like any demon; but her glance was sharp, so it bounced away from you: not soft, and treacherous as quicksand, like other demon eyes. Edie Mackintosh fed him, kept him safe, but Tom was almost sure she wasn't trying to enslave him. So what did she want?

At least the heat of the house was a little more bearable now, but he had a horrible feeling that was because his body temperature was rising. He was flushed with a constant, restless fever and the cool of the stars seemed farther away every moment. But then that might well be a good thing, as well, because he had another horrible feeling it was the stars that had destroyed the shed.

Tom's own room, where he'd spent the night, was horrible. It had blaring white walls and everything about it was irritating; but it was the best place to be because Edie Mackintosh left him alone there.

And it gave him a good view of next-door's garden.

Tom tilted his mirror so he could see out without having to go near the alder wreath that guarded the window. He was on the lookout for the Tribe — or else he was feasting his eyes on freedom — or . . . or else he was watching and watching for some other reason he wasn't sure about. The Tribe was quite likely to find him now, because they would have been alerted by his bringing down the anger of the stars upon the shed. But Tom spent more time gazing at the square shadow that was burned into the drenched grass than scanning the bare winter trees that might hide a slim figure with a silver spear.

The garden was empty for most of the afternoon.

The weather had turned to blustery rain that whipped the last few leaves from the trees. Tom sat for feverish hours in the bleaching heat of the house, watching.

A door banged, and he leaned forward towards the cool glass. It was Anna, looking even squatter from above. She plodded across the lawn to the black place where the shed had been and stood there for a moment. Her face was blotched with cold — pinched and woebegone. She made a careful circuit of the garden, peering under every bush and walking round both trees. Searching for something.

Tom knew what she was searching for. She walked slowly, sadly; and something about her cast a shadow into Tom's heart.

He sprang back in horror. No. No, it couldn't have happened. It was just a momentary thing — it would pass. It had passed already. She — it — had passed right out of his mind without leaving any trace, and he was still free.

She was walking round the sodden garden again. Her face was streaked with dirt where she had been crying.

Crying? Why did she cry when she wasn't injured?

But then she was a demon, a slave to all the other demons in the world. Any of their hurts might have made her cry.

Not that he cared, anyway.

But —

She was crying because he was gone.

Rage swept through him. The fool, to care about him when he was not even one of her kind. It was a disease with her, a compulsion. She'd care for anything — even the sophie. Always Anna was a fool. She'd been a fool to bring him food, shelter him, talk to him, save his life.

She was going back into the house now. Out of sight, out of mind.

She was gone, and he was himself again. Free.

He'd sit here and be glad she was gone, back into the house with the other foul demons.

But perhaps the others would drive her out again. He hoped —

No.

No.

Tom swung round away from the mirror and pressed his face against the cold wall. No. He called up a vision of the stars fighting — the glory of the freezing, swirling fire.

But the stars were outside himself, now — far away. Far away.

He thought of the Tribe, silver and beautiful. He thought of Sia. Tom's lips curled coldly, contemptuously. Next to Sia, Anna was heavy, lumpen, coarse. Anna was foolish, ignorant. Her face was red and her teeth were blunt.

But she was in his mind.

Tom cursed, gritted his teeth. He *would* be free of her. He would. He would not be her slave.

But her image was clinging to him, as sticky as a cobweb. The more he struggled to wipe it away the more he was smeared with it.

His hand.

Where Anna had touched it.

His sleeve.

Anna's was green.

Tom flung himself across the room and managed to push at the iron bar that opened the window. The damp, cold air blew in on him. Blow her away, he thought. Cool my heart.

The cold made Anna's nose revoltingly red.

No. Not be her slave. She was a fool, a fool, a fool, and he didn't care. He would curse her — destroy her. Send shafts of silver through her heart.

But — Tom felt tears rising in his own eyes, though he had no pain. It was as if Anna's tears had worn away channels inside him; and then he knew that he was too late, and she had been too cunning, and that she had bound them together. The cobweb between them was thickening and growing like a vine until he could feel it. He could feel it pulling against him. How could he bring down a curse on her now? He would be cursing himself.

Tom discovered that he hated her. He had hated before, but nothing like this. She had enslaved him and he would never be free again. He hated her and he hated her and hated her.

And he wondered when she would come out again.

30

An hour later the back door opened again, but it was Joe who came out this time. He was encumbered with a dustpan and brush and a sullen expression. He trudged up to the charred shadow of the shed, threw the dustpan down, and glared at it.

Anna followed him out and stood at an irresolute distance. Their voices came up clearly to Tom through the open window.

"What are you staring at?"

"Nothing."

"Then get lost."

Anna swayed, but her feet seemed too heavy to move. Tom gagged: it wasn't just himself that Anna had bound to her. She did the same to everybody, even Joe. *Even Joe.* Suddenly Tom hated Anna so much he could hardly breathe.

"Joe, where did you put all the stuff that was left over from the shed?"

"What's that got to do with you?"

"I just want to see it, that's all."

Joe kicked out moodily at the dustpan.

"Over by the compost heap. But there's nothing left."

Anna made her way over to the top of the garden and poked at things. Joe started sweeping up bits of molten glass. He trudged over to the trash can, tipped everything in, and trudged back for more.

"Joe!"

"What?"

"Is this everything?"

"Yep. And Dad says you're not to mess about with it because the insurance people haven't come yet."

Anna continued to hang around in a heavy, demonish, slave-making way, and Tom watched them. He wished he had a spear, and Larn's strength and skill to use it.

And then he was glad that he didn't.

"Joe!"

"Stop poking about or I'll tell Dad."

"You didn't find anything else?"

"Oh, get lost."

Anna plodded over and stood right in Joe's way.

"There wasn't anything you didn't tell Dad about?"

"I don't know what you —"

Anna stamped her foot. Wet bits of black splashed up onto Joe. He got up, exclaiming angrily, trying to brush them off.

"Yes, you do," said Anna. "You know what I mean. What else did you find?"

"Nothing! Nothing."

"Did you look everywhere?"

"Of course. I could hardly miss anything that big, could I?"

"What if he was invisible?"

Joe found that he was smearing black all over himself. He gave up and stood up straight.

"I felt around," he said, defensively. "He must have gone."

Joe turned away, but Anna went and stood in front of him again. How could she bear to be near *him*?

"How did it happen?"

Joe shrugged.

"I don't know. Everything just blew up."

"Why?"

"I told you, I don't know. You'll have to ask your pet pixie. If you can find him."

Anna stood quite still, thinking.

"Do you think it was one of the Tribe?"

"How should I know? It was probably Tom trying to kill me. And he got away."

"Or blown into a million pieces."

"Well, it's not my fault," said Joe irritably. "You don't think I encouraged him, do you? You don't think I said, *oh, and how about blasting the shed to smithereens*? I mean, that's what I really wanted, wasn't it, having my eyebrows burned off and having to explain to Dad and Evelyn why half the garden's exploded."

"Mum and Dad were really nice about it."

Joe shrugged.

"Anyway," said Anna, "you know Tom didn't want the shed blown up. He needed it so he could hide from his family. And he wasn't well."

Joe made a jeering noise. "How could you tell? He looked dead to start with."

"He had a fever. His temperature was right up to ten degrees the last time I took it."

"Well, perhaps he got delirious," said Joe sarcastically. "But I didn't have anything to do with it. All I did was get him to make himself invisible so —"

"Oh, you *idiot*!"

Joe threw down the dustpan and advanced on her. His ears were a dusky color, even more horrible than usual.

"You watch your —"

"I knew you'd done something. You bullied him into trying to reach the stars."

"Well, that's what I was supposed to be doing. Collecting evidence. That was the whole point of letting him stay in the shed."

Anna stared at him, suddenly white-faced, and her chest was heaving as if she'd been running a race.

"I hate you," she said, with a queer, quiet intensity. "I knew I should have found Tom somewhere to stay where you couldn't get at him."

"So what's the difference?" asked Joe, sneering. "He'd have gone anyway."

Anna clenched her stubby fists.

"But he'd be safe!" she burst out. "He could be anywhere — we know he's ill, and he's probably hurt as well. He's bound to be in all sorts of trouble."

Joe shrugged again.

"None of our business," he said.

And Anna hit him.

31

Demons had silly blunt teeth — but Tom would have thought they'd have been of some use in a fight. It wasn't as if they had tough skins.

Anna didn't have a clue how to kill someone. She was a lot smaller than Joe, but if she'd bitten his throat out straight away she'd have had a chance. As it was, Joe held her off with one hand while he jeered at her to make her even angrier.

Just for a moment, Tom wondered if he could knock down the alder wreath that hung above his window and slip down to help. He could come up behind Joe and strangle him with his belt.

But then Tom came to himself, and he cursed, long and thoroughly. It wasn't his fight. Joe and Anna were just shadows from his past — except that they weren't, because Anna had enslaved him. Tom screwed up his face and his fists and tried to drive her out of his mind.

He called up an image of the stars, and with their cold fire he tried to burn Anna out of his memory.

"Anna!"

Another voice. Tom forgot the stars and leaned close to the mirror. Now there was a third demon in the garden — Bernard. Bernard was on Anna in a huge brown swoop. It caught hold of her, but she was concentrating so hard on killing Joe she didn't realize it. She didn't realize it until Bernard had placed itself in front of her and got hold of her wrists.

That brought her to her senses. She was crying, and gasping, and making short bellowing noises through her teeth.

"Anna! What do you think you're *doing*?"

Bernard had to say it twice, the last time loud, before it got through to her.

"I'm trying to kill him!" she bellowed.

Joe was rubbing his hand resentfully.

"Vicious little rat," he said. "She needs a spanking."

Anna uttered a bloodcurdling howl and threw herself forward. She nearly pushed Bernard over the fence. He slipped on the winter mud, uttered a yelp, and just managed to keep his balance.

"Anna! Stop it!"

Joe was grinning at her.

"She needs to be sent to bed without her supper," he said.

Bernard caught Anna's arm, turned to Joe, and yelled, *"Shut up!"*

He could yell three times as loud as Anna. The noise echoed round the garden, and by the time it had finished Anna and Joe were staring at him, mouths wide open.

"For God's sake," Bernard went on, no longer bellowing, but hushed and fluttering, almost as if he'd managed to frighten himself. "What's going on? Anna, for crying out loud, love, what's the matter?"

Anna had to take several deep breaths before she'd calmed herself enough to speak.

"I hate him," she said tremulously.

"Who, Joe?"

She nodded, swallowing.

Bernard paused.

"It's a shame you lost your skateboard in the fire," he said. "And it's a big change having Joe here. But he said he's sorry. And he's part of the family, isn't he?"

Joe was grinning at her nastily.

"So be nice to me," he said.

Bernard took such a deep breath he almost left the ground. He didn't bellow this time, but it was clear he was only just holding it back.

"I said, *shut up!*"

Joe's face went blank with hatred.

Bernard and Joe stood, glaring, and Tom suddenly understood why it was that demons stared. They were each trying to gain control of the other, and staring made the bonds between them stronger. Yes, now that he knew the sort of thing he was looking for, he found he could see the vines that tied them. They were thin and sinewy, and they were pulling at them so hard it was a struggle for them to keep their balance.

At last Bernard gave a great sigh.

"Come on, Joe," he said. "I'm sorry I shouted, but it doesn't help to annoy Anna, does it?"

"At least I didn't hit her," said Joe tightly. "Look at my hand."

Bernard looked, and sighed.

"Anna —"

"I don't care," said Anna stoutly.

"Well *I* care," said Bernard. "We're here together, and we have to get along, don't we?"

"But I don't want him here," said Anna. "He's horrible and he — spoils everything."

"Well, you needn't think *I* want to be here," said Joe. "I'm only here because Mum decided she wanted to go off to New York without me."

"Now, now," said Bernard. "She didn't —"

"Yes, she did."

Bernard blinked several times.

"Well," he said, "well . . . er . . . it's nice that she's having a break for a few weeks. And I've been looking forward to you coming —"

Joe actually snarled.

"Oh yeah. I know how much you look forward to that. That's why you have me here all of twice a year, isn't it?"

Bernard cringed.

"Joe, that's — Look, Anna, love, I think Joe and I need to talk."

Anna snarled, then.

"Of course you do," she said. "It's always Joe, isn't it? You couldn't care less what I've got to say — it's always Joe who's right."

Bernard seemed to wilt.

"Anna —"

Anna turned swiftly to Joe.

"Dad may like you, but that's only because he doesn't know what you're really like. But I know you — and you're smelly and . . . and disgusting — and I'm never going to forgive you!"

And then she turned and stormed off.

32

Demons were massively strong, but by that time the vines hanging round Joe and Bernard were so thick Tom was surprised either of them could move. Tom could see other vines going in other directions, too, now that he had his eye in — some into the house, and others going off farther than he could see.

"Joe —" began Bernard heavily.

"Well?"

Bernard walked round in a circle and all the vines twisted and tightened and cut into his flesh.

"I'm sorry it's not much fun for you here," he said.

"*Much* fun?"

Bernard put up his arms as if to ward off the bitterness in Joe's words.

"Perhaps if we got you a bike," he began hopelessly. "Something to keep you occupied . . ."

Joe's teeth gleamed with contempt.

"You really haven't got a clue, have you."

Bernard shifted his weight from foot to foot, but the mass of vines kept him there.

"I don't suppose I have," he said dully. "You're growing up, Joe, and you're wanting to find your own way. And I can't help you with that — no one can. No matter how much I want to."

Bernard made a movement as if to put a hand on Joe's shoulder, but at the last moment he changed his mind. He walked away wearily, with the vines weighing him down, and Joe stared after him.

"Dad!"

Joe walked quickly down towards the house after him and out of sight.

It was as if he was pulled by a string that had suddenly thickened itself into a thick rope.

33

Tom stayed where he was, staring out at the empty garden. The alder wreath was jangling and fizzing, but he gritted his teeth and ignored it as best he could. Being in the house was like being in a box — he couldn't move, couldn't breathe. Perhaps he should jump out through the jangling of the wreath — take his chance.

But then suddenly a shadow fell over him. The sun, winter-weak, had got caught in a net of branches, but there was more to it than that. There was something new, very close. Something dangerous.

A sound on the landing made him jump round. There were fingers reaching round the shiny edge of his door.

Dry, bony fingers, with no heavy demon flesh about them.

Tom dived for the open window, but the jangling of

the alder wreath mounted into a wall of screaming sound that flung him back onto the bed.

And now there was a figure in the doorway, watching him. It was not beautiful, but withered by age. Not of the Tribe. Not of the Tribe.

"I thought I could feel a draft," it said. "Shut that window, can't you? I've got the heat going full blast. You might as well throw money away."

Edie stayed and watched him make the great teeth-clenched effort to push his arm through the jangling of the alder wreath to close the window. Then she nodded, and went away.

Tom lay flat on the bed, breathing hard. At least the old woman left him alone most of the time. At least she did not stare into his eyes, paw at him, try to step into his soul. The jangling was a little muted now the window was closed, but he could still feel a shadow in the room, like a silver shaft of ice.

He heaved himself up on one elbow and then, in the mirror, he spotted it. The fingers of another hand were reaching round the trunk of next-door's apple tree. Thin fingers, they were, with no hint of demon flesh about them.

Lured by cold; lured by fire.

Tom drew back quickly into the shadows, watching. And above the clutching fingers appeared an oval face, and then, black in the dusk like bitter sloes, a pair of almond eyes.

Hunting eyes.

34

Edie Mackintosh came into his room the next morning with another hoop of alder. She tied it to the curtain rail above the window.

"There," she said. "That cheers up the room a bit, doesn't it?"

Tom did not think so. This one was still damp and new and tinged with green algae, and it fizzed and jangled so loud that he couldn't think.

He spent the morning huddled into a corner of his room as far from the alder wreath and the radiator as he could get. Leaning against the cold wall drew some of the heat out of him, for his smoldering fever had burned away the chill of Larn's coming.

Sometimes he found the strength to watch next-door's garden in the mirror. It was drizzling, and he longed to be out in the cool rain. But he was even more trapped than ever now: trapped by the heat that was burning away every sense he had, and trapped by the alder twigs that were shaking his brain into confusion; but trapped most of all by those hunting eyes.

Anna came out into the garden once, trudging through the rain. She went all round, searching, and in the end she left something white on a plate under a bush.

And then Joe came out to join her and they trudged off together along the side path and down to the road. They were hazy with tugging vines.

They returned two hours later, frozen and miserable, heads down. Tom wondered very much what had happened between them, and this helped distract his mind a little from the flooding heat and the nerve-screaming jangling of the alder wreaths.

He hardly saw Edie Mackintosh all that morning, but as she was in the kitchen preparing their food, she began to sing. Her voice was blaring — coarse and uncouth, lurching about without grace. At first. But as she sang her voice grew clearer. She sang a tune he'd never heard before — but somehow, far away, it had an echo of Tribe-song about it.

The Queen o'Fairies she caught me,
In yon green hill to dwell . . .

He knew the words, too: it was the story of Tam Lin, who had been captured by the Tribe, and of the demon Janet, who won him back and had his child. Tom listened greedily, half soothed, half disturbed.

During the last part of the song Edie Mackintosh's voice went very, very high.

35

✷ In both gardens the wet clothes hung sullenly in the lowering afternoon, as damp as they ever had been and threatening to freeze. Edie had given Tom a huge mound of steaming demon-stuff for lunch. He'd eaten it — but three-quarters of the way through he'd realized for the first time ever that it might be possible to eat so much that you stopped wanting to eat any more.

He went back to his room to wait for the overstuffed feeling to wear off, but the heat of the food inside him was so strong he found himself breathless and gasping like a stranded fish. He clenched his teeth, thrust his hand through the vibrations of the alder wreath, and flung the window wide.

The cold, damp air closed on his face and he took a great gulp of fresh air.

There was someone in the garden next door. It was a full-grown female — fat, she was, even for a demon. She was taking the clothes down from the line.

And there was another pair of eyes watching her too.

Larn. He was curled at ease in a tree, and anyone who couldn't sense his chill would never have spotted him. Tom drew back quickly behind his curtain.

But at that moment it wasn't Tom that Larn was hunting. All his attention was on the demon woman. He was watching her attentively — even though she was purple and fat and her hands were red and there was no beauty about her at all.

But then there was a commotion on the path between the two houses. And when Tom looked back Larn had gone.

"You two look as though you need something warm to drink," said the fat female demon as Joe and Anna came out of the passageway.

That was a trick to ensnare them, and it worked. The vines between them thickened and shortened and brought them to her.

"What've you been doing all this time?"

"Looking round the town," said Joe dismally.

The demon gave a sad laugh.

"I'm afraid it's not very exciting compared with London," she said. "Did you take Joe to the Sports Center, Anna?"

"We went up on the common," said Anna.

"Well, no wonder you're so muddy. What did you want to go up there for?"

"We were looking for a friend," said Anna. "But he wasn't there."

"Oh dear," said the fat demon comfortably. "You should have arranged to meet at the Sports Center. I'll tell you what, I'll give you some money tomorrow and then you can go swimming. Did you bring your trunks, Joe?"

"I don't like swimming," said Joe morosely.

The fat demon took two shirts off the line. Then she tried again.

"Perhaps your friend got the time muddled up," she said. "You should have asked him here. You're always welcome to use the phone, Joe."

Anna kicked out at the basket.

"We couldn't. We don't know his number and we don't know where he lives."

"Oh dear," said the fat demon again. "So where did you meet him?"

"Just hanging round," said Anna.

"You should have asked him in," said the fat demon. Then she suddenly stopped in the act of folding a clammy sweater. "Would that be the boy Edie spoke to me about? She said that she'd seen someone hanging around."

Joe and Anna looked at each other.

"That might be him," admitted Joe reluctantly.

"Well, you can be sure Edie will have nosed out all there is to know about him. She and Frank — Frank was her husband, Joe, such a lovely man — they were always taking in children who needed a place to stay. A really devoted couple, they were. Hasn't Edie said anything to you?"

Anna suddenly frowned.

"I haven't talked to her for a day or two," she said.

The fat demon blinked her fleshy eyes.

"Well, that makes a change. I suppose she must have been busy. What did she say when you came down the pathway just now?"

"We got by without her seeing us," answered Anna slowly.

The fat demon looked puzzled and a little worried.

"I hope she's not ill," she said. "It's not like her to let anyone go up the path without popping out. I better go round and see how she is."

"No," said Joe suddenly. "It's all right, Evelyn. I'll go with Anna."

"But —" began Anna.

"— because it *is* funny, isn't it?" went on Joe, meaningly. "That Edie shouldn't come out to see what we're up to."

"I suppose so," said Anna thoughtfully. "It's almost as if —"

"Yes," said Joe. "Isn't it?"

The fat demon looked from one to the other of them.

"Well, as long as *you* know what you're talking about," she said. "All right, go and knock on her door, then. But change out of those muddy shoes first. And don't be too long, or you'll be late for dinner."

36

Someone hit the front door twice. That was what you did when you wanted to get into a demon's house. Tom stood in the dimness at the top of the stairs and waited.

They'd changed their shoes, but their hair was still starry with mist.

Edie looked them up and down and nodded.

"I thought it would be you two," she said. "You'd better come in."

They edged in sideways.

"I suppose you're looking for your friend," said Edie.

"Well —"

"Tom!"

The vines that Anna had cast over him pulled him so hard that he stumbled on the stairs.

She went dusky pink when she saw him. Revolting — but suddenly Tom felt as if he was in the right place. Joe was scowling at the carpet.

131

Edie stood with her hands on her hips.

"He won't talk," she said, with a jerk of her head at Tom. "Not a word all the time he's been here. I've told him he's going to have to talk sometime. We've already had a mad-doctor round — and I won't be able to put off taking him to see a medical doctor much longer, and he won't be able to fool *him*."

Anna and Joe didn't seem able to think of anything to say.

Edie sniffed at them.

"Well, as you're here," she said, "you can do something useful."

She took her great padded coat off a peg and thrust a thin arm through the sleeve. It jingled strangely as she settled it on her shoulder.

"I've got to go to the supermarket," she said. "Stay here and look after him. I shouldn't be more than half an hour, as long as the car starts."

Tom stepped back hurriedly from the dim cold that came in through the door. Larn might be out there.

Edie turned back in the doorway, adjusting her stiff, bowl-shaped hat.

"Don't you try and take him out, whatever you do,"

she said. "He's safe here — or as safe as he can be. I've got all the doors and windows so nothing bad can get in."

"What sort of thing?" asked Joe, as jeering as he dared.

Edie snorted.

"Tom knows," she said, and banged the door behind her.

You could never feel safe with demons: the moment the door was shut Anna threw herself at him. He stepped back quickly, but the wooden post at the bottom of the stairs got in the way and he couldn't dodge her heavy arms. It was so horrible he almost bit her.

"Oh, Tom," said Anna, sighing foul demon smells all over him. "Oh, I'm so glad you're safe."

Tom shuddered down and out under her elbow.

"You are all right, aren't you?" she went on, pursuing him, peering at him from her bulging eyes. "You aren't hurt?"

Tom backed into the sitting room and slid himself into a corner behind a stuffed armchair. He felt safer there. Anna and Joe stood in the doorway.

"I am not injured," he said.

"I'm really glad," said Anna. "We both are." She nudged Joe, who wriggled his shoulders and swung himself uncomfortably from foot to foot.

"Yeah," he said. "Look — when I made you — well, I didn't mean the shed to blow up. Especially not with me in it."

"And we both still really want to help you," said Anna. "Don't we, Joe?"

"Yeah," muttered Joe ungraciously.

"So you just tell us anything we can do. Anything you need help with."

Tom wished he understood her. Anna had already enslaved him. What more did she want?

"I think I am dying," he said. And it wasn't until that moment that he realized it was true. For a long time, and especially since he'd been in this house, his senses had been decaying. First his hearing, and then his eyesight, and now it was as if his whole self, mind and body, was being dried up in the heat of this dreadful house.

"Oh," said Joe, blankly. "Er . . . right."

"We could take him to the hospital," suggested Anna doubtfully. "I've got enough money for the bus fares."

"Yeah," said Joe, "and what do you think they'd make of someone with a normal temperature below zero?"

"Well — I suppose they could do tests and things."

Tom's stomach turned over at the thought of those tests. Anyway —

"I cannot leave the house," he said. He gestured at the hoop of alder twigs that hung from the curtain rail. "I cannot easily pass a ring of alder."

Joe wandered thoughtfully up to the alder wreath. He showed no sign of being affected by it.

"What if I took it down?" he asked. "Could you go out then?"

"Yes. But then the others of the Tribe could come in, and they would kill me."

"So you get killed if you go out, and you die if you stay in," said Joe. "Difficult."

Anna was wandering round the room.

"We could call a taxi," she said. "Or . . . perhaps Tom's got it all wrong. I don't suppose his parents could really want to kill him."

Demons were just so stupid. Tom lowered himself wearily onto the arm of a chair.

"My sire has found me. I have seen him. He is hunting me."

"How would he kill you?" asked Joe, fascinated.

"With a spear, probably. Unless he got a chance to throttle me. That would give him more satisfaction, I think."

Anna shivered.

"I can't believe it," she said. "No one could really be like that. Not so they *enjoy* killing."

Joe gave half a laugh.

"Oh, yes, they could," he said. "It's fun. I remember stamping on frogs in the park once. It was really good. I know I screamed like mad the next week because they'd all gone, and — *that's it!*"

"I'm glad I made Dad put a padlock on Sophie's hutch," said Anna with distaste, and Tom wondered why Joe had *stamped* on the frogs. They were much better as they were, with the bones still crunchy.

Joe was suddenly red with excitement.

"That's how we can stop Tom's parents trying to kill him!"

"How?" asked Anna.

Joe smirked

"Easy," he said. "We'll kill him ourselves."

37

"What we'll do," said Joe, "is get Tom's clothes and smear lots of blood on them, and leave them on the common. And then the Tribe will think he's been killed by wild animals."

Demons were stupid.

"There is nothing on the common that would eat me," Tom objected. "Not skull and all."

But Joe was entranced by the brilliance of his idea.

"You could die some other way, then," he said. "Under a train. We could leave your clothes at the side of the railway line, and they'd go all stiff with ice, like a corpse, and then the Tribe will think —"

"The Tribe will think you're stupid," said a dry voice behind him.

Edie was standing watching them.

There was a stunned, stomach-somersaulting moment of silence. Then Anna managed to find her voice.

"We were — we were playing a game," she said foolishly; and Edie snorted.

"I should think so. The idea that a silly trick like that would fool the Tribe. Tom'll tell you."

Tom felt a whole series of shudders running through him.

"What Tribe?" demanded Joe hoarsely.

Edie put three string shopping bags on the table.

"Why, the fair folk that live on the common, of course. Now you listen to me. I've got him pretty safe in here with all these wreaths of alder guarding the entrances. I don't say none of the fair folk could get past — but they could only do it if they helped each other, and I can't see that happening. No, they're a sour-souled lot, are the Tribe."

Joe was making bad-taste faces.

"Look," he said, rather aggrieved. "How come you know about the Tribe?"

Edie snorted again.

"Because I've lived here all my life, that's why. You can't live on the edge of a dangerous place like the common without knowing something about it."

"But . . . I've lived here all my life, too," said Anna. "And no one's said anything to me."

Edie hesitated, then slowly pulled out a chair and sat down.

"People nowadays haven't got much sense," she said. "In the old days everyone learned about the Tribe. They sang songs about them at school. Everyone may have pretended the words were made-up stories, but they knew all right."

"Knew what?" asked Joe, but only half contemptuously.

"Never to go to the common alone. Never to look at one of the Tribe. Never to look back. To beware of moonlight."

"What's wrong with moonlight?" asked Joe uneasily.

"You tell him," said Edie Mackintosh.

"It's easier to be invisible in moonlight," said Tom. "The Tribe sometimes comes right into the city, then."

"What city?"

"This city," said Tom. "Here."

There was a pause while Anna and Joe digested this.

"So are there quite often members of the Tribe in town?" asked Joe, at last.

"That's right," said Edie.

"Well, in that case they can't be very dangerous, can

they? I mean, you don't often hear of people being found impaled with silver spears, do you?"

Edie hissed at him.

"Of course not. The fair folk aren't looking to kill people. What would be the good in that?"

"Then . . . what do they want?" asked Anna.

Edie looked down at her worn hands.

"They want them alive," she said.

38

There was silence in the room until the echo of the last words had died away. Then Joe spoke.

"You're putting us on," he said. "If it was true then they'd have concreted the whole common over and put barbed wire round."

"Do you think that the fair folk don't know that? That's why they move quietly. But they still move, I can assure you of that. Have you never heard of anyone disappearing?"

"Only Tom," said Joe. "Anyway, it's impossible. According to quantum theory —"

"Not like that!" snapped Edie. "Not vanishing in a puff of smoke! I mean *disappearing*. Have you never heard of a person leaving home and never being seen again?"

There was another pause. Then:

"I have heard of that," said Anna quietly. "There was someone —"

But Joe swept all that aside.

"They go to London," he said. "They have arguments with their parents and go to London or Newcastle or somewhere and get jobs."

"Not all of them," said Edie. "Some don't get so far. That's mostly the young, handsome ones. One of the fair folk will lure them in."

"And then what?" demanded Joe. "What happens to them?"

"The bones of the fair folk never linger long: perhaps the bodies of those they've finished with go the same way. To the stars."

Joe scowled.

"You're making it all up."

Edie pushed herself to her feet.

"You ask Tom," she said. "All I'm saying is, he's safer in the house."

"But he's not," said Anna. "He's ill. And he's getting worse."

Edie shrugged.

"Nothing I can do about that."

"And —" Anna seemed to be wrestling with something difficult. "Even if he was all right — you can't keep him in the house forever, can you?"

"Can't I?"

Anna wrinkled her forehead.

"Well —"

"Because I'll tell you this," said Edie dryly. "I doubt he'll live very long after he leaves."

39

The straining growl of Edie's car receded once more into the late afternoon gloom.

"It's all right," whispered Joe. "She's turned the corner."

"We're coming!"

Joe had already taken down the alder wreath that hung over the side door. It was only three steps across the passageway to the door to Anna's house.

"It'll be all right," said Anna, from behind Tom. "Joe's shut the back gate, and he's blocked off the other way with bits of the shed. It's quite safe. Come on. You might feel better in our house."

Tom could feel the heat of her beating on his back. He took a step away from her, and into the chill dusk.

"Don't stop," said Anna, ushering him forward protectively.

Tom stepped over the threshold of Anna's house. It felt quite different from Edie Mackintosh's. And it certainly *smelled* different.

"It's the garlic," said Anna, seeing his nose twitch. "I've put garlic purée on some paper plates and stuck them to the windows. It's all right, I asked Dad when he was too busy unpacking his train set to be bothered to argue. It's to keep the Tribe away."

Joe loomed up out of the darkness. He rolled his eyes upwards.

"That's *vampires*," he said. "It's vampires that don't like garlic."

"Well, the Tribe might be the same sort of thing as vampires."

"You're daft. The Tribe *likes* silver, so they can't be."

"Oh. I never thought of that." Anna sighed. "Oh well, it can't do any harm."

"You should have given Tom the garlic," said Joe. "That'd keep everyone away from him."

Bernard came into the room carrying a length of something curved and metallic.

"Have you got that sandpaper?" he asked Joe. "We'll have to get all this rust off."

"Dad, this is Tom," said Joe. "He's staying next door with Edie Mackintosh."

Bernard nodded.

All the furniture in the next room was pushed

against a wall and the floor was covered in metallic strips and tiny boxes on wheels. Bernard was so heavy he had trouble getting down on the floor. It was clear he'd have even more trouble getting up, and that made Tom feel quite a bit safer.

"Here we are," said Joe. "There's two pieces."

"Oh, good. Do you think you could do that straight bit?"

There was a box in the corner of the room with a web of wire across the front. There was something alive in it. The sophie.

"This is where we keep her," said Anna. "Would you like to hold her?"

Tom shook his head. He was feeling too peculiar even to want to eat her: and he still didn't understand why Anna kept a piece of meat in the house. There was no point in making a *slave* of an animal. Was there?

Anna led Tom to an armchair and perched herself on the edge of it.

"Dad's got his train set down and they're pretending they're fixing it so they can sell it," she whispered. "Mum says it's a male bonding thing. How are you? Are you feeling any better in here?"

Tom sat and breathed. It was a help to have got away from the alder wreaths. He was still drenched with heat, but now that he was away from the constant jangling he could think straight at last. But — He looked across at Bernard and Joe. They were rubbing away at their pieces of metal; they weren't looking at each other or exchanging a word, but as Tom looked a new thick vine was forming between them, as heavy as a chain. And now it was growing again, out towards his chair. It caught Anna first; and he could hardly believe it didn't weigh her down to the ground. All she did was lie back against the padded chair like a cat in the sunshine.

The great shadowy vine kept on growing. It put out a tendril and Tom had to move his leg quite sharply to avoid it. But it followed him, relentlessly. A great thick vine that would tie him — bind him — to all these demons.

He wriggled swiftly out of his chair before it could corner him.

"Are you all right?" asked Anna.

The vine swerved in its path. Being tied to Anna was bad enough — but if this great heavy thing got him it'd crush all the life out of him.

The vine was blocking his way to the door. Tom looked around. There was a window. That would do.

"Tom," said Anna. "Tom, what's the matter?"

He felt round the window frame. It was constructed differently from the one in his room at Edie Mackintosh's.

"Tom, do you want me to open the window?"

That was Anna, fussing. Demons all fussed. They bound themselves together so they could hardly move, and then they wondered why it was so difficult for them to do anything. Anna even bound herself to animals like the sophie. He felt a spurt of anger at all demons. They were disgusting — fat and smelly and red and gross.

"Tom —"

He couldn't work out how to open the window. Stupid demons with their stupid possessions. He hated them all. Hated them.

Anna put a hand on his arm, but he sidestepped. She looked dark — shadowy with the vines that tied her to the others. No wonder demons were so massive — they had to be to bear the weight of all the vines that bound them.

He stood at bay, with a great vine reaching out for him — hating so fiercely — and as he did, the great vine reaching for him died. It shrivelled and turned black as if a cruel frost had collapsed its veins.

And Tom stood there, free.

All the demons were staring at him from their cocoon of vine-growth: but he didn't have to care about them any more. He was free of them all. Triumphant, he stepped forwards towards the door and the vine shriveled before him.

"Is Tom all right?" asked Bernard. "He's gone so pale."

Joe was sitting up, alert and alarmed.

"I think he wants to go home," he said. "He can get a bit . . . er . . . shy, sometimes. Anna, I think you'd better show him out."

Anna slipped through into the kitchen and opened the back door.

"I'll watch you back to Edie's," she whispered. "And I'll look in later on to make sure you're all right."

Bernard was saying: "Funny sort of a lad, isn't he?"

It was damp outside, and cool. Tom breathed deep. It was real fresh air that wasn't tainted with demons or demon things. Free air.

"Hurry up," Anna whispered. "You never know who might be lurking about. And we don't want Edie coming back and catching you out of the house."

She opened Edie Mackintosh's back door and took down the alder wreath so he could go through.

But he wasn't going back in there. That house smothered him, dissolved him, drove him mad. He couldn't go back in there, skulking in a demon house while all his senses drained away, while he died.

It was quite dark; the moon was rising, full and beautiful and splendid. It would be turning the soft darkness of the common into a stippled tangle of black and silver.

Anna shivered.

"I wouldn't hang around out here," she said. "It's freezing, and there's moonlight as well. Look, if you like, I'll come in with you and wait for Edie to come back."

Tom could feel the air of Edie Mackintosh's house coming out at him, stale and vibrating, drying his flesh, destroying his mind. He stood and hated Anna, and Joe, and everything else; every demon thing in this demon city that was killing him.

The stars were far away. Tom looked up at them and he knew that however loud he called, they would not hear him.

But they were still beautiful, even without his true sight. He could not see it now, but they were fighting.

Always the stars were fighting — because that was the price of freedom.

Suddenly it was as if the Tribe was before him. He saw them sliced by the moonlight; separate, silver clad, full of pride and triumph.

Through Edie's door he could see the square white box upon which she scorched her food. And he thought of the stag, slit, with its warm blood spilled onto the tough grass.

Demon eyes did not see well in the dark.

"Tom?" said Anna. "Tom, where are you going? Tom, it's dangerous for you to be outside. Tom!"

But Tom was free of her at last.

40

The cold air was like wine. Tom slipped down to the end of the road and turned downhill, towards the river. Suddenly, he knew what he wanted.

At the edge of town was the bridge. Tom went on with no thought but of getting away from the smell of the city of the demons and back to the common. Getting home. He cared nothing for the chariots that swerved hard cones of light through him. And then there was blackness, soft blackness, and that was the common; the place to which he would always return.

He kicked off his sterile demon slippers and stepped onto the grass. There were stones under his feet and he was part of the common again. Demons walked apart from the world — skin, eyes, ears, all shut away.

The blackness was open, velvety. He plunged into it.

Everywhere was dark — or perhaps he'd been away so long he'd lost his woodcraft. He tripped over something, cursed, and a swinging bramble caught at his neck. Then he had to stop and unhook the thorns to get free.

He needed to watch where he was going — but he couldn't. That was the trouble. The moon was there, but it had lost its potency — or he had lost half his sight — for he found himself blundering through a cruel net of whipping branches that snatched at him and tripped him and forced him around so that if it hadn't been for the steady moon he would have lost all sense of direction.

He emerged at last, panting, into a place where there was grass under his feet.

Help me, he whispered to the diamond-hard stars: but the cold air caught his words and scattered them.

He turned to follow the grassy trail. He knew the common — knew every inch — but this place seemed strange. He couldn't see it well, but it *smelled* wrong — at least, didn't smell much of anything.

And then he tripped on something — something that caught at his ankle — and as he fell he thought of Anna.

He thrust her away. Anna was the past. She had happened. That was all. The past was a foreign country, separate from today. *The past casts no shadows;* that was what they said. Out of sight, out of mind. He would not think of demons. He hated them, hated them, hated them.

And as he hated, the vine let go its hold.

Tom took a deep breath of free air. It rinsed away Anna, and Joe, and Edie Mackintosh; and then he was free again.

The common was busy with shadows and shafts of silver moonlight.

He listened. Nothing. No one. Alone. That was a word of power: he was stronger even than the Tribe, because he was completely alone. He would travel north, and then farther. It would be easy because he had no fear of demons. He would live off them — raid their trash cans and steal their pets.

Anna?

He staggered, caught by the throat this time. Another vine. Well, he could get rid of that. Anna was a little fool. A fool from the past who had nothing to do with him. She would soon have forgotten him. He would wither all the vines that tied him to her. Now they were separate. Separate.

He raised his hands to the sky and laughed. He was even free of the stars. The Tribe was bogged down —

he laughed triumphantly, squeezing the mud between his toes — bogged down on the common. They were trapped by demons. The Tribe thought they were free, but they lived in fear, which was not freedom at all. He had spent his whole life in fear, in hiding. Not living at all.

Tom went on through the wood. This would be the last time.

Far away a demon chariot swooped along the road. Demons had the best of it: he could see it now. They were slaves; but at least they were happy in their slavery.

Like Anna?

This time the vines came at him from two directions at once, pinioning his arms, and for a moment it was hard to hate: all he could do was remember. Tom remembered the touch of Anna's hand. Her eyes. And then, like a flower opening, at last he knew that Anna had not wanted him as her slave. She had been trying to tell him — but he didn't know what she had been trying to tell him. Give him. He was almost sure she had been trying to give him something.

But she was a demon, hot and coarse and heavy. And he hated her. Hated her. *Hated her.*

The vines withered and fell.

He walked on a little farther and the jagged stripes of black and silver made way for him.

And then he came to a clearing.

He saw Sia first, and her beauty smote him. He had forgotten: forgotten the turn of her head and the grace of her body.

None of the Tribe took notice of him. Larn was there, too, with his spear resting on his shoulder and on the bend of his knee. The moonlight caught the hollows of his skull and lay shimmering on his fair hair.

And then one of the Tribe raised a voice in song. And Tom knew the song.

O I forbid you, maidens all
That wear gold in your hair
To come or go by Carterhaugh
For young Tam Lin is there.

41

★ The song spun a spell so that it no longer seemed a song, but a ribbon of pictures before his eyes. He saw the golden-haired she-demon who went wandering in the wild places, and the beautiful young man she took for her lover. He had heard the story a thousand times; he had always liked the part where Tam Lin changed into an adder best.

But now a different part of the story caught him, a part he had hardly noticed before. For there was an extra person in the story. When the golden-haired demon had come back to claim Tam Lin for her own, she was expecting his child.

Before him, in the ribbon of pictures conjured up by the song, he saw a butterfly dance across a meadow.

A butterfly.

And now the song was telling of the anger of the Tribe-woman who had lost Tam Lin. A terrible curse she spoke, to turn Tam Lin's eyes to wood. And she cursed the she-demon, too.

> *Shame betide her ill-fared face*
> *And an ill death may she die,*
> *For she's taken away the bonniest knight*
> *In all my company.*

A butterfly.

The she-demon was expecting Tam Lin's child — but perhaps there had been other children, too: Tam Lin, the bonny knight, had lived with the Tribe for seven years.

What would those children have been, with a demon sire, but calved into the Tribe? Demon? Or of the Tribe?

Or something else.

The song came to an end and the ribbon of light faded and expired, and the Tribe was before him again. He could not see them whole, but the moon carved lines of brightness that highlighted a cheek or an arm.

What would they be like, those children? Would some of them have not grown their fangs? Would they have stared and clung and cried? Would they have called on the stars?

What would the Tribe have done with calves like that?

A butterfly. An egg, a caterpillar, a chrysalis, a butterfly. What if some of those children had started all right, but had begun to lose their sight and hearing as they grew older? Changing, as everything changed. One day Larn would lose some of his skill, and then one of the younger ones would kill him and take over his hunting ground.

Would Joe kill Bernard, in the same way?

Of course not. They were too entwined to do each other harm. Joe had tried to hate the others, but he couldn't do it. No one could, living among demons. He'd been caught by their relentless vines.

Caught and tied down so he couldn't move, couldn't think. So he lost himself.

The moon rose and the shadows of the Tribe shortened. Tom looked at Sia, who was so beautiful. He didn't hate her. The Tribe seemed like a painting to him: not real at all.

He wasn't one of the Tribe.

I'll go away, he thought. Live alone.

Alone. Free. Perhaps after a little while —

Tom started to hurt in a way that was new to him. It

started heavy on his chest, and then it tightened his throat. He couldn't live like the Tribe — hating and fighting: it was beautiful, and splendid; but it was impossible.

He did not fit. Not with demons and their smothering vines, not with the Tribe. He was alone. Alone.

He stood and breathed. His head was suddenly quite clear: he didn't want the Tribe, or demons, or himself. And the stars were out of reach.

There was only one thing he wanted.

He took three paces forward and he stood before the Tribe.

42

In an instant every eye was on Tom. Then the Tribe stirred, and suddenly there was only Larn, standing before him with his spear in his hand; and the Tribe had vanished except for a brief movement of the air and the chill of hunting eyes all around him. And in the moonlight the trees were like a cage.

Tom waited. He waited for the rest of his life — but that was only a little while.

Larn pulled back his arm — so elegant he was, so beautiful — and then he was still for a moment, balanced and perfect. Tom looked down at the spear and it only seemed a few inches long. How strange, Tom thought: how glad I am that this is the end.

Larn thrust.

Somewhere, a voice shouted — but the spear had hit him, and entered him, and the stars came lower, and they were swirling with fire.

The spear was icy cold inside him, and now the world was fading. But still there were the stars.

And now other things were round him — warm things. Demons, perhaps. And they had hold of him, and their warm arms helped soothe the searing cold of the spear.

"Did you see that?" said someone: someone close, but also far away.

"I'm not sure what I saw. Tom? *Tom!*"

"It looked — for a moment I thought there was a whole circle of people among the trees — and one of them had a spear. That's why I shouted."

"He's not answering. Joe, why isn't he answering?"

"This moonlight makes everything so tricky. Tom, can you hear me?"

"We'll have to get him home."

"I know. Help me turn him over and we'll see if we can carry him."

The stars were all around Tom now, fiery and cold. They joined with the coldness of the spear. But the warmth of the demons was there, too. And it was all interesting and pleasant; and he was not afraid.

"Oh, God!"

They'd turned him on his back. Their hands were on his chest. But he could not see anything except the brightness of the flaring stars.

"I can't touch it. Anna, I can see it, sort of, but I can't touch it!"

"It's a spear. A silver spear. That's — that's what Tom was afraid of all the time."

"What can we do?"

And then a new voice spoke behind them.

"It's too late to do anything," it said. "All we can do now is remember him."

43

⭐ Joe and Anna. Tom remembered those voices; and the other voice was not strange. Icy flames licked around him, and he felt at peace.

"Edie Mackintosh!"

"How did you get here?"

Edie. That was right.

"How do you think?"

Another pair of hands. Cool, these ones were, not like clammy demon hands at all. But there was hot water splashing down on his face through the flames.

"What are you crying for?" asked Edie roughly.

A face came down near Tom's.

"He's still breathing. If you drove down to find a phone and called an ambulance —"

Someone was wrapping him in something.

"That wouldn't do any good."

"But —"

"All the science in the hospital wouldn't help him. You know that."

"But . . . then . . . if we got some herbs or something —"

"Said a spell —"

"Got hold of one of the Tribe —"

Edie laughed. Tom heard it and was glad.

"The Tribe? They're already here."

"What?"

"Can't you feel them all around? *Don't look!* It's dangerous to look."

"But if I caught one of them —"

"You might as well try to catch the moonshine. And it wouldn't be any good. Tom's got a Tribe-spear through his heart. He's dying. He's beyond the reach of any medicine."

Warm hands paddled at him.

"Tom!"

Anna's voice. The flames of the stars were dimming, now, into a soft and luminous haze. It was very comfortable: but he was at the bottom of a deep well, and he was too far away to answer.

"Tom!"

Her voice was full of pain, and Tom was sorry. But the stars had gone; and the light was dimming.

44

⁎ Joe clenched his fists as he knelt in the frozen mud.

"We must do *something*," he muttered.

Anna closed her cupped hands tightly around the spear that erupted so horribly from Tom's chest. But her hands closed on nothing.

"I don't understand," said Joe. His face was white, but his voice was so loud and rough that it did not waver. He passed his hand through the spear. "I can see it," he said doggedly. "So it must be there."

Anna put her face down close beside Tom's.

"Tom, it's Anna," she whispered urgently. "Tom, it isn't a *real* spear. Please wake up."

"It's real enough," said Joe. "But it's Tribe, so we can't sense it properly. Perhaps if we could — I don't know — work out how to think like the Tribe —"

"You're wasting your time," said Edie Mackintosh, who was standing with her back against a tree.

Anna screwed up her face with effort.

"Coldness . . . and moonlight —"

"— and being alone," said Joe. "Being all alone with everyone hating you. Everyone who comes near you wants something from you. Wants to hurt you."

"And the stars," said Anna. "The stars are important. They reach out and take you if you ask them hard enough. And they are fierce and beautiful."

Joe turned his face upwards.

"Like diamonds," he said. "Stars! *Take me into your world!*"

He sat very still, breathing softly. Then he reached out for the spear — but his hand passed through it again.

"There's no point in making faces," said Edie Mackintosh. "That won't help."

Joe swung towards her, very angry.

"At least I'm trying! Why don't *you* try? We can't just give up. Can we?"

"Why not?"

The hard, high words were flung at him scornfully.

"He has nothing to do with you," Edie said. "The Tribe hates you. Anyway, you don't know anything about it. The stars aren't diamonds to the Tribe, they're big and low and they fill the sky with hatred and with fire."

"Don't," said Anna miserably, without lifting her head. "Don't fight. Not now. Please don't fight."

The moonlight carved black gashes round Edie Mackintosh's mouth and made wells of shadow out of which her pale eyes glowed. She nodded curtly.

"Anna's right," she said. "It's not worth fighting over. He'll be dead soon, and then everything'll be back to normal."

Anna made a small stricken cry and Joe scrambled to his feet, even angrier than before — but then suddenly something caught his eye, and he looked past Edie Mackintosh.

And he froze, openmouthed.

45

"Don't look!" said Edie, sharply. "Never look at one of the Tribe. Joe, did you hear me?"

Anna was pulling the coat more tightly around Tom. "Tom can't be going to die," she whispered.

Joe's gaze was fixed, like a sleepwalker's, on something behind Edie.

"He can't be," Anna whispered. "Because he *does* have something to do with me. When I met him he was hurt and all alone — he was so alone —"

"Joe, you mustn't."

Joe began to walk forward, but Edie caught his arm.

"She's trying to lure you away."

"Tom," said Anna, and suddenly her voice was strong and clear. "You can't leave me. Not now. You're part of me now. And *I won't let you go.*"

Edie, with sudden strength, swung Joe right round.

"You'll bring down half the Tribe on you!" she said. "If you're captured by a Tribe-woman then the men will all be out for your blood. Come back to us, Joe. Look at your sister. Look at Anna."

Joe swayed, and blinked, and held up a hand against the dazzle of the moonlight.

Then suddenly he staggered and went down on his knees. He began frantically pushing at his arms and legs as if he was trying to escape from the clutches of some many-armed beast.

"No," he muttered. "I won't. I won't. Let me go. *I want to be free!*"

But then he fell forward onto his hands and knees.

Anna's voice came again, and it rang, triumphant, through the wood.

"Both of you will stay," she said. "Because *you both belong to me.*"

And Joe, trying desperately to breathe against the clutching black vines, saw a tendril looping and twining round the spear that was in Tom's chest.

But then there was a shadow on the ground in front of him, and it was like a tall man. And something leaped at him like a flash of lightning — but it was cold, so cold — and it passed through Joe's heart, and the lights went out.

46

✴ Tom's peace broke away — gone, it was, in a moment. And then it was as if he was falling hard and fast: and the earth hit him, jarred him, nearly broke his bones. And it was dark. Darker than he'd ever known.

And the stars were gone.

And now there were voices Tom had never heard before — neither high Tribe voices nor blaring demons' — but yet somehow they were not strange.

Something was shaking him. His back scraped the ground — and the earth was harder than it had ever been before. One voice was higher than the others, and harder, but somehow it chimed in his heart. Tom turned his head with a huge, swollen, leaden effort.

"Joe!" said the hard voice. Its hardness made it clear; made it race like a spear into Tom's body. "Joe, can you hear me? Joe!"

And a shape beside Tom stirred and whimpered and turned.

There were the stars. Tom could see them. Tiny pin-pricks of silver far, far away. So very far away.

He lifted his right hand. It was heavy — very heavy — although the black silhouette against the near-blackness of the sky was the same as it had always been.

"Tom's moving! Oh Edie, he's moving!"

And then over Tom's memory came something that he didn't understand. There was something . . . somebody —

"Anna," said Tom. And his voice was strange, too. Not Tribe. But not demon, either. It was a middle voice, a little like Anna's.

And he found himself glad it was like Anna's.

Something took hold of his hand.

"You've come back," it said. "Oh, Tom, I'm glad you've come back!"

But he wasn't back at all. This was a different place. Unless the world was the same and it was he that was different.

Yes. That was what had happened. He was a new person, and everything he had ever known was gone. Everything except Anna; and someone beside him who held his head and groaned; and someone with a hard voice.

He turned to them for comfort.

172

47

Tom opened his eyes to Edie Mackintosh's cold back room. He felt impossibly heavy, so he lay and looked around him. The white walls had gone dingy cream — but then everything everywhere had changed color: even his skin had gone from white to a sort of biscuit color.

It was all horrible, so he closed his eyes.

Anna came to see him, later, when Edie Mackintosh had pestered him into getting dressed and coming downstairs.

"Oh!" Anna said, standing and staring. "Tom?"

Edie Mackintosh gave her a small push to get her out of the doorway.

"Of course it's Tom," she said. "Who else?"

Tom sat in his chair, still so very heavy, and was glad she'd come.

"Something's happened to everybody," he explained. He'd almost stopped being surprised by his new voice, and was beginning to like it. "You've all stopped being demons."

"I wasn't ever a demon," said Anna. "Though I must admit it's an easy mistake to make as far as Joe's concerned."

"How is he?" asked Edie Mackintosh.

"He's a bit quiet. But he's coming once he's finished his breakfast."

There was a knock on the door as she spoke and Edie went to answer it.

"Is Tom all right?"

"Come in and see him."

Joe looked different, just as everyone else looked different. There was a new shadow in his eyes, a wariness. But perhaps that had always been there.

Joe stood and stared at Tom for a long time.

"You're not one of the Tribe anymore," he said, at last.

Tom knew that was true. True beyond fighting, true beyond hope.

"Everyone changes, Joe," said Edie, almost gently. "All of us, all the time."

Anna nodded wisely.

"Dad even says that if we're all really, really nice to you then eventually you might turn out all right, for a boy," she said.

Joe looked at her and something about his face changed. It was as if the person who was hidden away in fear looked out for a moment.

"Well, I might," he said. "If you're really, really nice to me."

48

The world was full of demons; but they were nothing to fear, mostly, except perhaps for the ones who were very stupid or unhappy. Millions upon millions of demons living together, interlinked, but mostly not unhappy.

Very odd, that was. Odd, but pleasant, once you got used to the idea.

Families. That was how it worked. Every calf — child — was born into a family. It was so simple: if a calf had someone to protect it, then it didn't have to fight for itself. It was only when it trusted no one that it had to fight.

Tom tried to explain this idea to Anna and Joe. Anna had taken it upon herself to give him lessons in being human, and Joe liked to hang around and annoy her. Being human was even more complicated than Tom had thought: Anna just went on and on and *on*.

By the third day he'd had enough.

"But I will never be a real human," he blurted out into the middle of an endless list of instructions. "I will be too horrible."

"What?" asked Anna, startled.

"Horrible," repeated Tom. "Like Joe."

Anna gave a yelp of joy and Joe sat up in tall indignation.

"I'm not horrible," he protested.

"Like you used to be," amended Tom.

Joe opened his mouth, thought for a moment, and then sat back again.

"What makes you think you'll be horrible?"

"Because demon calves — children — need someone particular to be their slave, to protect them. And I have no one particular."

Edie Mackintosh was clattering about in the kitchen making cups of tea. That was another thing: humans made their drinks so hot they couldn't drink them. They also had a habit of flavoring the water with dried-up leaves. Tom was trying to get used to it, but it still seemed a lot simpler to lap up water from puddles.

Edie Mackintosh was singing as she waited for the kettle to boil. She often sang when she was working — not loudly, but absentmindedly, under her breath. She was singing the song of the demon Tam Lin again, who'd been captured by the elven queen and lived with her for seven years.

They sat and listened. Edie's voice was pure and very, very high.

"Not exactly in the Top Forty, is it," said Joe, yawning. "I bet that song's even older than Frank Sinatra."

"But of course it is," said Anna suddenly. "The Tribe and humans have been living beside each other for hundreds of years. That's it."

"What?" asked Joe sleepily, but Anna didn't answer him.

"Tom, what was your aunt's name?"

It took Tom a little time to work it out. These demon relationship words sat uneasily when they were applied to the Tribe.

"Edrin," he said, at last.

"And what happened to her?"

Tom was overtaken by a memory of darkness. He shivered.

"I told you. It was Larn — he killed her."

"With a spear. He'd have killed her with a spear, wouldn't he?"

Joe was suddenly sitting up and wide awake.

"Of course," he said. "Of course, of course! He killed her — just like he killed Tom. Just like —"

Edie Mackintosh came in with a tray bearing four steaming mugs.

"Here we are," she said. "What are you lot staring at?"

Anna got up and went and placed her fingers gently against Edie's cheek.

"You're cold," she said.

Edie Mackintosh set down the tray.

"Poor circulation," she said. "Lots of people suffer from it as they get older."

Joe got up too.

"And you're so very thin, too," he said. "You're the thinnest person I've ever seen. I think — except for Tom."

Edie Mackintosh flicked him irritably with a dish towel.

"Don't be so rude."

Tom looked at her eyes. They were flecked with lights. Silver lights. He held his breath, because he knew he was within a hairsbreadth of discovering something of tremendous importance.

The three children were circling her now, delicately and silently, as one would some great marvel.

"Because it doesn't work, does it?" said Joe triumphantly. "Larn's spear. It didn't kill Tom."

"Well, it doesn't take a genius to work that out," said Edie, grumbling.

"Yes," said Anna, her eyes shining. "Larn's spear is part of the Tribe's world: it can kill animals, because they live half in the Tribe world anyway; and it can kill one of the Tribe."

"But some members of the Tribe are different," went on Joe. "Like Tom was different. As they grow up, they change. First they are clumsy, and then their hearing fails, and then their sight, until at last they are a danger to the Tribe and they have to be killed."

Tom knew then. He even knew why he had been drawn to this particular part of this demon city.

Like attracts like.

He stepped up to Edie Mackintosh and looked into her face. Her skin was aged, no longer glowing, but still he could trace the delicate bones of her skull. And her fierce eyes had seen many things.

"Why didn't Larn's spear kill you?" he asked.

Edie Mackintosh stepped away from him and sat down, quite suddenly, her hands clutched to her heart.

"That was . . . another person," she said. "Long ago. Long ago. Frank tried to pull it out — Frank who became my husband. He was a good man. But he couldn't touch it. I would have gone to my death — dancing with the stars — but Frank wouldn't let me; wouldn't let me be at peace. The stars were all around me, but he kept shouting at me, shouting and screaming — and in the end the stars faded and everything went black. And when I woke up I was back at his house, and somehow I wasn't dead; and I was a different person."

Dancing with the stars. Yes. That was right. Tom suddenly found himself full of joy. Not fighting, but dancing. The stars had always been dancing. Not hating, but . . . something else.

The world was a different place.

Anna knelt down and took hold of Edie's hands.

"You are Edrin, aren't you?"

But the old woman shook her head.

"No. Not now. Not now. I'm someone else."

There was a silence. And then Anna said:

"Why didn't you tell us? Why didn't you tell Tom,

especially? You knew what he was from the very beginning, didn't you?"

Edie nodded slowly.

"I could feel the cold of him," she said, "and I was afraid that the Tribe was on my track at last. But then, when the stars took the shed, there was only me to help him: and when I saw him I knew he was one like me, Tribe, but not Tribe. And so I kept him as safe as I could, waited to see if the Tribe part of him would fade, called in those who would allow me to keep him, let him find his own way. Made sure he never knew I was afraid: for he was Tribe. I know I've lived a long time, but I've no desire to die till I have to. No desire to wake in the night with fingers at my throat, or feel a spear in my back. So I've always worn a hard hat — makes me look a fool, but there's worse things than that — and we made a chain lining for my coat, Frank and I. And I drive everywhere. I feel safe in my car. We decided that we'd never tell anyone where I'd come from; it was safest, for one thing, and for another — the Tribe — I didn't want to destroy it."

Tom understood that.

"The Tribe is very beautiful," he said.

"You get used to the fear," Edie said to him softly. "It's always there, but you get used to it."

"But you don't have to be afraid," said Joe suddenly. "You're human now. Larn can't hurt you."

Edie shook her head.

"Larn's spear nearly killed me. I don't know why it didn't, unless Frank saved me somehow. That's why I was doing my best to provoke you last night — I wanted to make you angry like Frank had been angry. There wasn't anything else I could do."

Joe frowned ferociously.

"But it was the creeper that saved Tom," he said. He stopped and looked round at all their blank faces. "Didn't you see? There was a woman —"

"You forget all about that," said Edie Mackintosh. "That wasn't for you."

"— and when I saw her suddenly the wood got brighter. And she called me — I think she did, anyway, only I can't remember her saying anything — but then suddenly Tom and Anna were in front of me, and they had big vines, big creepers tying them together. And then one of the creepers caught me, and another one twined round the spear. And . . . I think . . . there was a man . . . and he threw something cold, like lightning, that went through me. I *think* it was a spear. But it didn't hurt really, except to make the wood go dark again."

A vine. Tom took a deep, tremulous breath. That was what had saved him, and what had saved Edrin before him. The strength of the slave-bonds between him and Anna had dragged him into the demon world; and now he'd never be free. Never.

"So there's no need to be afraid," went on Joe, triumphantly. "You're both human now; and a Tribe spear can't hurt you, any more than it hurt me."

"But . . . the Tribe . . . they can still cast spells over humans," said Anna hesitantly. "Call us away into their world, like the woman you saw did to you."

Then Edie laughed.

"I'm much too old for the Tribe to be interested in that," she said. "And Tom's too young as yet."

"So you're safe," said Joe. "You could even go up on the common. The Tribe can't hurt you."

Tom and Edie looked at each other.

"Safe?" said Edie softly; and her silver-flecked eyes went suddenly deep, like moonlight on a pond. "With this changeling in this house? That's the last thing I feel. But I would be glad to walk on the common again."

Anna was walking round the room.

"These children," she asked, peering at the little photographs. "Are these *all* yours?"

"Well, we weren't expecting children, what with one thing and another," said Edie. "And when the first one came along we were so pleased I think we got a bit carried away."

Joe was trying to match up the pictures.

"Three boys," he said. "How many girls?"

"Another three," admitted Edie. "But the last two were twins. And that one there's Jason, he was one I fostered. And fourteen grandchildren, so far. And another one on the way."

Joe screwed up his face.

"And none of them are completely human," he said. "Interesting. And if the Tribe can lure humans into their own world, like in the story of Tam Lin, there must be human bits — genes, I suppose — among the Tribe, too — and that's why sometimes members of the Tribe start developing human characteristics as they grow up."

Anna nodded.

"But human genes come out stronger in the end, and that's why there are so few of the Tribe," she said.

They all sat in silence for a little while.

"I wonder how many humans have a bit of Tribe in them?" said Joe suddenly. "I bet I've got some Tribe in me. I bet that's why I could see that Tribe-woman."

"I shouldn't be surprised," said Edie dryly.

Anna smiled at Tom.

"Anyway, you've got loads of family," she said. "Twenty cousins."

"And another one on the way," put in Edie smugly.

"And an aunt," said Joe.

Tom walked round the little pictures. There were so many of them. And soon vines would grow out of their bodies and bind him to them forever and ever in the same way that he was bound to Edie and Anna and Joe.

Suddenly he wanted to run away — to be free. To find that lonely moor and live by trapping and gleaning, all alone.

But it wasn't going to happen. The vines were invisible now, but they were still there, tying him to the others. He was trapped. Trapped forever.

There must have been something stricken about his face, because Anna took his hand.

"We'll help," she said, and he quailed in the light of her eyes. Suddenly he could hardly breathe against the weight of all those demon vines. He was one demon among all the millions, now — and all those millions would control him every second he was alive.

Well, his bones were thick and strong. He would live. Or, at any rate, he would not die. He would dance, along with all the others.

Dance forever as a demon slave.

Suddenly he remembered how beautiful Sia was: but Anna was talking, and the vine that joined them together was pulling that vision away.